The Case of the Empty Tomb

To STU - A GREAT GUY!
HERE'S SOMETHING
TO READ ON THE LONG
DARK NIGHTS IN
GERALDTON.

THANKS

THE CASE OF THE EMPTY TOMB

Tribune Claudius Maximus

Stephen Gaspar

iUniverse, Inc.

New York Lincoln Shanghai

The Case of the Empty Tomb

Tribune Claudius Maximus

iUniverse, Inc.

For information address:
iUniverse, Inc.
2021 Pine Lake Road, Suite 100
Lincoln, NE 68512
www.iuniverse.com

Author Photo Credit by John Pike.

ISBN: 0-595-31459-7

Printed in the United States of America

This book is dedicated to Father Paul Charbonneau,

who had more faith in me than I had in myself.

I would like to thank my loving wife Susan,

who is the first reader of all my work,

and Aimee Parent who helped edit this book.

CHAPTER I

▼

I hated the desert. I hated the heat, and the sand, and the dust. I hated everything about it. To me, the desert was nothing but a barren wasteland—lifeless, arid, and deadly. The desert held no hope, no life, no chance for life. It reminded me of man's soul, if one tended to believe in that sort of thing. All of Judea was nothing but a vast burned over desert, conducive to nothing, and supporting no life except for snakes, scorpions and Hebrews.

I missed Rome. I missed Rome so much I was beginning to dream about it in my sleep. I missed the festivals and the Forum, the tributes and the temples. I missed our family home in the city, and our home in the country, the one by the sea, where, as a boy I would sit and watch the waves for hours. I loved the sea. I loved the way it smelled, and how the spray felt on my face, and the sound of breakers crashing against the shore. I loved its blue-green colour, its pulsating tides, the waves and whitecaps.

Judea was desert country populated by desert people. Here the people raised sheep and goats, listened to desert prophets, and worshipped a mysterious god.

Jerusalem in the spring. The almond trees had lost their blooms, and the barley harvest had just begun. The rains were ending, and soon the dry season would begin. Just four days ago Jerusalem experienced harsh weather—the sky clouded over rather quickly, it rained for a time, and I thought I heard thunder. Now today was sunny and bright. Strange weather. Strange country. Strange days. I dearly missed Rome. Thinking of Rome made my heart ache. Here I was, banished to Judea, living on the edge of a desert in the middle of nowhere, with not a clue as to when I could return to—as the poet put it—my *alma mater*. I suppose things could have been worse, but at the time I could not see how.

By the way, my name is Maximus, Claudius Maximus. I'm a tribune.

It was a clear morning on *dies Martis*—Tuesday—after the ides of *Aprilis* when I received word to report to Praetor Lucius Servanus. I was not looking forward to seeing him. Servanus and I had a love/hate relationship—he did not love me, and I hated him. Servanus made me feel *magni nominis umbra*—as if I were living in the shadow of a great name. The trouble was, I knew it was only too true. The Praetor appeared to be his usual self today—a mean, angry man with a perpetual scowl whose manner made you imagine he was ready to cut off your ears.

"You look as if you've been dragged through Hades!" he greeted me—and I was wearing my best toga. "When I call to see someone, I expect them to come immediately. What kept you?"

"Traffic in the street was heavy," I said.

"Wise-ass. I do not like you, Maximus."

"Your secret is safe with me."

His beady brown eyes narrowed and his pudgy face puckered. "That is the exact attitude that got you banished from Rome and sent here."

"My attitude is not what got me here," I told him with an edge like flint.

Lucius Servanus took one step back. He reconsidered his position and withdrew from his verbal assault. The Praetor walked slowly to his desk and shuffled some papers uneasily. After he allowed sufficient time to pass, he began the conversation again, in a more subdued, professional manner.

"A situation has come to our attention." he said.

Translation: the powers that be had a problem.

"We want you to look into it."

Translation: they wanted me to handle their problem.

"We trust you to deal with the situation to your utmost ability as a son of Rome."

Translation: the problem was now totally my responsibility. I was to prevent any scandal that would reflect poorly on Rome and her officials. If anything went wrong, it would be my neck, and my neck alone left sticking out to be lopped off.

That was the way it always went. Whenever high officials stepped in a mess, they called Claudius Maximus to clean it up.

"What is the situation?" I asked, feigning interest.

Lucius Servanus let out a long breath and motioned to the only two chairs in the room. He adjusted his toga in a dignified manner and sat. We sat directly opposite of one another four paces apart. Any closer and it would have appeared that we were friends.

"Were you present at the last crucifixion?" he asked me.

I endeavoured to look thoughtful. "The last one was…when?"

"Four—no, five days ago, *dies verneris*—Friday last. Did you witness it?"

"I was otherwise occupied," I remarked, and Servanus gave me a nasty sneer that revealed his displeasure.

"Three Hebrews were crucified that day," the Praetor continued. "Two were common thieves. The third man was a Galilean."

Servanus thrust his head forward as if prompting my recollection. I shrugged to show that I did not.

"The man was a political dissident, an enemy of Rome, and was duly executed." The Praetor spoke as if trying to convince me, or himself. He paused a long moment, but somehow I knew there was more. "This Hebrew was no ordinary dissident. He made some fantastic claims while he lived. The man was obviously disturbed."

"What did he say?"

"Nonsense mostly. He said he was the son of God. He actually proclaimed himself king of the Jews."

I nodded, but did not respond. Jerusalem was not that large that I had not heard rumours about these claims. Of course, I had not put any stock in the stories I had heard regarding a Galilean I had never seen.

"It is also reported that he made an inane claim that he would rise from the dead." The Praetor let this last statement dangle. I decided to let it hang there while Servanus took two deep breaths to compose himself.

"We have received reports that the Galilean's body is missing from its tomb. *Fama volat.* This rumour has led people—Hebrews mostly—to claim they have actually seen the man *post mortem*. We want you to look into the matter. The man had followers—disciples. We do not wish to see the problem get out of hand. *Cessante causa cessat et effectus*—the cause ceasing, the effect also ceases. Recover the body so we can lay this matter to rest and expose it as some ridiculous hoax. Bring forward the ones responsible to answer for their actions."

"Is that all?" I asked.

"That is all," Servanus said rising from his chair.

I remained sitting and asked: "Did this political dissident from Galilee have a name?"

Servanus shuffled through some papers on his desk, picked one out and studied it. "The man's name was…Jesus," he said, squinting at the report. "Jesus of Nazareth."

I rose and turned to leave when Servanus added, "The Governor has taken a special interest in this case. He wishes to see it brought to its inevitable conclusion. He will not tolerate failure, and neither will I."

I nodded my understanding, and took my leave. The Praetor's last words were too apparent. If this did not go well, the chances of my ever returning to Rome were negligible.

Back in my quarters I removed my toga which I wore only on official meetings—the one with Servanus barely counted—and I went out in my tunic. I felt it made my appearance less conspicuous. I walked out of the Antonia Fortress that served as the barracks for the Roman troops in Jerusalem. The structure, built by Herod the Great, was named after his then-patron, Mark Antony. The name of the fortress no longer carried the respect it once did. Soon after his defeat by Octavian's forces, Antony took his own life like any dishonoured Roman should. With its massive walls and four tall towers the fortress was a grand structure by Judean standards, and was situated in the northeast corner of Jerusalem.

Outside, the bright sun reflected off the white stone of the fortress. To keep from under the hot sun I stood in the shadow of the archway. From there, I looked south over the city. Jerusalem was a vast collection of sun-dried buildings housing some sixty thousand inhabitants. Out there, somewhere, I needed to find a least one person who knew where the body of the Galilean, Jesus was taken. Not a very appealing prospect, but I was not in a position to be particular. Considering how my life started out, things could not look more dismal. Sometimes life is funny, and sometimes it is so ridiculous you have to laugh or you'll cry. Right then, I did not know which I wanted to do more.

CHAPTER II

▼

The first step in my investigation was to visit Meshullam Malachi, a Hebrew elder, scholar and philosopher, and perhaps the only friend I had in all Jerusalem. I was not certain why Malachi and I had struck up such a quick friendship—me being a young Roman Tribune of twenty-eight, and he a Hebrew elder of sixty-seven. Perhaps it was that we both shared Roman citizenship, neither of us being native of Judea, both outcasts from the lands of our birth. Maybe it was because both he and I knew that things were never as simple as they seemed. We were both men of the world and did not cling to any of the superstitions and steadfast beliefs other did. Not that Malachi did not believe in his religion, it was simply that he did not have to go about proving it to others every day like a Pharisee.

I descended the long, wide stairs of the Antonia Fortress and entered the market area in the city's lowest ravine referred to as the Valley of the Cheesemakers. The market appeared remarkably crowded and busy today, due mainly to the fact that this was the Hebrews' largest public festival—Passover, they called it. At this time of year Jerusalem saw an incredible influx of Hebrews from all over the world, as pilgrims swarmed into the city to celebrate an ancient tradition. During the seven-day festival, the Jewish population had swelled to four times its number, and I, for one, was pleased that these pilgrims would soon be leaving the city and returning to their homeland. The last thing Jerusalem needed was more Jews.

I passed the seemingly endless stalls where merchants hawked their wares and haggled with customers as if their very lives depended on making a bargain. The market was noisy with activity, and the smells of fruits and vegetables mingled with the aromas of spices and perfumes—not always a pleasant mixture. I pushed my way through the hurly-burly detecting foreign accents and spotting pilgrims from their different style of dress. They stood out on the streets of Jerusalem as much as I did.

I purchased some sun-dried grapes for breakfast and stuffed them into my mouth as I walked south through the city. To my left, adjoining the fortress, stood the mighty walls of the Temple Mount, and beyond the walls in the middle of a spacious court surrounded by stone balustrades with pinnacles, stood the mysterious Temple. The Temple was the centre of life for the Hebrews and the sole reason the pilgrims had come to Jerusalem. There were more Jews in the rest of the world than there were in the entire country I would wager, and all of them, both foreign and domestic, payed tithes to the Temple. I walked beside the long wall of large square-cut stones that led to a viaduct. Passing under the viaduct that cut across the city from east to west and connected the Temple Mount to the Citadel, I entered the Upper City. Here lived Jerusalem's elite, the rich, the influential, the elders and priests. Here also was the modest home of Meshullam Malachi. It was not generally acceptable for Jews to be seen associating with non-Jews, so Malachi and I set up a system so we could meet and talk *sub rosa*. In his home I greeted him by his Greco-Roman name of Marcus because I knew he did not like it.

"Greetings, young Maximus," he replied showing no offence. He was a handsome man, for an old Hebrew, with a long, straight nose that was more Greek than Roman, and a large, flexible mouth. His long grey hair matched his beard, but his most notable features were his green eyes that looked as they must have when he was a young man—vital and sharp. The deep lines on his face betrayed his age and reflected great wisdom. I found him dressed in robes common to his people, though understated for one of his station. It was a plain white ankle-length, seamless tunic tied at the waist by a long girdle. Malachi seldom smiled openly, but there was still honour and mirth hidden there on his face. The man was Thracian by birth, educated in Jerusalem as a boy, and in the rest of the world as a man. He spoke a dozen languages and knew practically everything. In my position he was indispensable to me.

"You are well?" he asked sincerely.

"I am as well as I can be," I answered. "And how are things?"

"Things are as they are. What brings the Roman Tribune Maximus to my humble abode?"

"I am in need of your services."

"My services are that of a teacher. Have you come to learn?"

I nodded.

"I teach men the ways of the Hebrew faith," he said. "Have you come to learn the Hebrew faith?"

"Partly."

"One does not learn *part* of the Hebrew faith, my young friend. It is all or nothing."

I said, "I have a problem."

"As always."

"I need information."

"As always."

"I am in need of information that only you can provide," I began the litany. "If you can aid me in this, I will be humbly in your debt."

There was a hint of a smile on his lips as he heard the words he was waiting for.

"Tribune Maximus, my limited knowledge is at your service. How may I aid you and the Roman Empire?"

Sometimes Malachi put on displays of servitude—the conquered serving the conqueror, but we both knew he took undue pleasure in seeing a Roman ask a Hebrew for aid. Moreover, it made him feel useful, and gave him the opportunity to display his remarkable mind.

"What can you tell me of a man called Jesus of Nazareth?" I asked plainly.

Malachi's face grew a little sterner, and said just as plainly: "He is dead. You Romans crucified him."

"That much I know. What else can you tell me about him?"

The old man paused briefly. From his demeanour, I—who knew him better than even he imagined—could see that his mind was recalling information, and was preparing to bring it forth like a fountain spouts out water.

"Born in Bethlehem to a good family. Father was a tradesman—now deceased. Mother is a very holy woman. Jesus lived in Nazareth most of his life. There is nothing remarkable about his early years. About three years ago he began a life as a teacher and developed a quick following. His teachings were ridiculed in the Hebrew community. Some say he blasphemed and taught heresy. He more often could be found amongst known sinners than with respectable, God-fearing people. Some uncorroborated accounts state that he performed miracles of healing. Still other say his teachings opposed the word of God."

"Did he?"

"Did he what?"

"Did Jesus go against the word of God?" I asked.

"Basically he did—according to the letter of the law."

"You Hebrews and your law," I remarked with a chuckle.

"Our law," Malachi said with conviction, "which was passed down to us from Moses, who, in turn, received them from God, is all we have! It is who we are! Rome has many laws. Where would the Roman Empire be without them?"

I felt that I had struck a nerve, and made a mental note never to do it again.

"Did the Hebrew elders see Jesus's teachings as a serious infraction of your law?" I asked.

"Yes," he replied simply, but it was in the way he answered that told me there was something more. "The elders considered some of the Galilean's teaching as blasphemous," he added.

"And that is serious?"

Marcus Malachi looked me in the eye, then turned away and said slightly abashed, "The penalty for blasphemy is death."

I looked back at him, surprised, and repeated, "Death? That seems quite harsh."

He nodded. "I did not say it was easy being Hebrew. We have come to understand *dura lex sed lex*—the law is hard but it is the law."

I nodded in understanding.

"You stated that legally Jesus spoke against God's law," I said in a calm tone. "Do you believe that to be true?"

The old man studied me intently. This conversation had arisen before. He wanted me to understand that the law was the law. But the law was interpreted by men, he had once told me in confidence, and whereas God was infallible, men were not. Some law was open to interpretation. Malachi had argued in the past with high priests and elders regarding their law. He learned to be discreet in his teachings and how he interpreted the law. He had not been so discreet in Thrace, and it was this indiscretion that brought about his banishment.

"I heard Jesus speak in the Temple once," he told me with a combination of sadness and admiration. "Later I had the opportunity to converse with him."

"And?"

"A very charismatic young man. He was only around thirty years of age. I could not help but see something in him—something unique. Not that all of his teachings were unique, but his views were different. *Non nova sed nove*—not new things but in a new way. He put things in such a simple manner that they were difficult to refute. The more complicated you proposed a viewpoint or problem, the more simple he would make it."

"Your people boast of producing prophets, Malachi. Was Jesus simply another prophet?"

"Perhaps he was," he uttered. "But his teachings were not shared by the elders and high priests. He had made enemies in the Sanhedrin. And as you know, young Maximus, although Jerusalem is under the occupation of Rome, the Sanhedrin tribunal holds authority over Hebrew religious and legal disputes."

"Yes," I said thoughtfully, "but tell me, Marcus, to whom do you owe allegiance, the Sadducees or the Pharisees?"

"You know I do not choose sides in the tribunal," he stated. "I find the rift between the two groups only weaken us as a nation. The differences between the Pharisees and the Sadducees are minor. Unfortunately they continue to argue their petty points, instead of tending to the welfare of the people."

"Was that view also shared by Jesus?" I queried.

He nodded and said, "I believe so."

I shook my head in incomprehension. "What is the point of it all?" I asked. "Will you people ever change?"

Malachi drew back as if struck. "There is no way I can make you understand what it is to be Hebrew," he said. "Our beliefs date back to Abraham. They are beliefs and traditions hallowed by time, honed through practice, past on by generations. It is what links us to the past and binds us to the one true God. You smile. Have I said something to amuse you?"

"It is strange to hear you speak this way. I did not believe you were encumbered by superstition."

"Make no mistake, Tribune"—he called me tribune. He wished to remind me that I was Roman and he was Hebrew, and that there were certain lines we could not cross. "Despite the Roman citizenship I inherited from my father, I am first and foremost Hebrew. My faith and my beliefs are two other things I also inherited from my father, who inherited them from his father all the way back to Abraham. I could no more deny them than I could the nose on my face. It is who I am."

"Point taken," I said. "But did the Sanhedrin consider Jesus a threat?"

"The elders and priests took it as an insult when Jesus challenged them on teachings they spent their entire lives studying. Pride is a fragile thing to a man. Arrogance grows from it. It is not easy for a learned man to admit he has more to learn. We are teachers—we do not wish to be taught. To many of us on the Sanhedrin, it was clear Jesus was a traitor to his people and his beliefs. Rome had to be convinced he was their enemy also."

"How much of that do you believe?" I asked.

"I do not know," he said sadly. "I will tell you this; I have come to believe that if the teachings are of man, then they will go the way of all men. But if the teachings are of God…" His voice trailed off and I was left to draw my own conclusions.

"Jesus had garnered as many enemies as he did followers," Marcus Malachi continued. "It seemed that both the Pharisees and the Herodians were hostile towards him."

"Why would the followers of the tetrarch Herod be against Jesus?" I asked.

"I am not certain," Marcus murmured then said, "But even Jesus's own followers proved they were not to be trusted, it seemed. One of his own delivered Jesus into the power of the elders and the Sanhedrin. Subsequently he was brought before Caiaphas, then the Governor, Pilate, who sent Jesus to Herod, who sent him back to Pilate. I was not certain if no one wanted to charge Jesus, or simply if everyone wanted a part in bringing the man down. Finally Jesus was sentenced to death and was crucified."

Malachi ended abruptly and I tried to absorb it all.

After a time he asked: "What is your interest in the Galilean, my young friend?"

"The body of Jesus is missing from its tomb."

"Oh?"

"And there have been accounts—rumours actually—that the man is not dead."

I expected some kind of response from Marcus, but he only nodded his head.

"Have you heard anything regarding these claims?" I asked.

"Yes," he said. "Word of this has reached me."

"What do you make of it all?"

He took in a long breath and let it out. "The woman who made this claim was one of his followers, and is not very reliable. I would not call her an upstanding member of the community. She has a reputation."

I took his meaning and nodded. "Who is she?"

"Her name is Mary Magdalene."

"Who would have taken the body, Marcus? His followers?"

"There is that possibility."

"But why?"

"To substantiate the man's claim that the Spirit of the Lord was upon him and he was the appointed by God."

"Did the man actually said that?" I asked a little dumbfounded.

"The tribunal asked Jesus if he was the son of God, and he said, 'It is right that you say I am.' He spoke of God as if He were his father and their relationship was intimate. If the followers of Jesus took the body from the tomb, it might have been to prove his deity."

"Now this is beginning to make some sense," I remarked. "They took the body to perpetuate the myth, and began rumours about his rising from the dead and actually seeing him alive."

"Yes," said Marcus. "That certainly seems a viable theory." But I heard doubt in his voice.

"You do not believe they took his body, do you?"

"Maximus, I neither believe nor disbelieve matters I have not explored thoroughly."

"All I have to do is track down these followers, get them to show me where they hid the body and expose it as a hoax. Simple."

"Good luck, my friend," he told me sincerely. "I am curious as to what your investigation will uncover."

CHAPTER III

▼

I was pleased this case was going to be a simple one. I was in no mood for a long, drawn out, and complicated investigation. The sooner I could return to my quarters the better.

I took my leave of Marcus Malachi and left the Upper City. The sun beat down as if roasting Jerusalem, and the sickly smells of the city grew heavy and made my head swim. Walking north, I passed under the viaduct through a different street than I had come, and made my way to the city gate in the western wall. Passing through the gate, I saw Calvary across the road. The locals referred to it as Golgotha, the place of the skull, and it was here public executions took place. Poles—or *stipes*—stuck out of the ground waiting for their victims to come bearing the crosspiece—or *patibulum*—that would be fixed to the *stipe*. The condemned would then be tied or nailed hands and feet to the cross. Crucifixion was a strong deterrent to prevent civil disobedience, and no one ever seemed to question its results. As I stared at these grim, silent sentinels, they seemed to say: *memento mori*—remember that you will die. I turned away from them and walked north. The road sloped down and it met another road that led me below Calvary. There I faced a rock wall that led straight up to the posts I had just seen. Looking up at the rough rock facing, I could see how the place got its name, for there in the coarse rock were features that resembled a human skull. Two deep hollows made up a pair of empty eye sockets. Between the hollows, a pointed stone stuck out like a nose, and below that, the rock remarkably resembled a downcast mouth and jutting chin. It seemed appropriate. It was a place of death. Close by were small caves where the dead were buried. Before I had a chance to look for the empty tomb that once held the body of Jesus the Galilean, I became aware of two men approaching. I stood still and slowly eased into a cleft to remain undetected.

The two men were older, about fifty years of age, and both were Hebrew. From their manner of dress I could tell they were members of the Sanhedrin, one a Sadducee and the other a Pharisee, the two sects that vied for religious control in Jerusalem. I thought it strange that they were here together. Their actions seemed mysterious and conspiratorial. Both appeared agitated and distressed, so much so that they did not even observe me as they passed close by.

"He is gone, I tell you!" said the well-dressed Sadducee.

"How can that be?" asked the other.

"Come see for yourself!" the Sadducee told his companion. "The stone has been rolled away and the tomb is empty!"

"Is it possible?"

"If it happened, it is possible."

I followed them as they walked north along the rock wall. I had no fear of being seen. They appeared so intent on their mission that they would not have noticed me had I walked beside them. A short walk led us to a garden. The two men stopped before the opening of a tomb cut into solid rock. They stood there for a brief time before ducking inside. I approached the opening silently and stood listening. From inside their voices reached my ears, muffled and low. Taking a deep breath, I followed them into the tomb. It was a small cave and low, so low in fact I had to remain stooped over. The cave had a strange smell, but I was certain it was not death I smelled. I had smelled death before, and this was not the scent I remembered. The two men, startled by my sudden appearance, jumped and cried out as if I were a spirit.

"What are the two of you doing here?" I asked authoritatively.

Both were struck momentarily dumb as they clutched at their hearts and looked guilty.

Again I demanded to know the reason for their presence.

"This is my tomb," the Sadducee finally managed to utter.

"And who are you?" I asked.

"My name—" he began.

"Wait," I said as an uneasiness crept over me. "Let us go outside. I do not care to question you in this place."

The three of us walked out into the hot light of day.

"Now," I said, "who are you?"

"My name is Joseph, I am from Arimathea, and this is my tomb."

The man was dressed in rich clothes of white, trimmed at the collar and cuff with detailed embroidery.

"And you?" I said turning to the Pharisee.

"My name is Nicodemus," he replied with some resentment. The man's dress was simpler than that of his companion, and was trimmed with fringes and tassels. "Who are you?"

"I ask the questions here!" I stated boldly. "I am Tribune Claudius Maximus, and I am looking for the body of Jesus of Nazareth." The two exchanged uneasy glances. "This is his tomb, is it not?"

"No," Joseph of Arimathea proclaimed. "This is my tomb."

"Do not lie to me!" I shouted, and took a threatening step towards him.

"No, no, Tribune," said Nicodemus coming forward to defend his companion. "Joseph is telling the truth. This is his tomb."

"Then what were the two of you talking about moments ago when you said, 'he is gone, the tomb is empty.'"

The pair looked at me amazed as if I had performed some type of strange alchemy. Then their faces drew down with a look of defeat.

"Very well, Tribune, we will tell you," began Joseph. "Jesus of Nazareth was buried here, but I spoke the truth when I said it was my tomb. I purchased this cave some time ago, and when Jesus was crucified I arranged for his body to be placed in here." He gestured to the cave.

"Why would you do that?"

"I knew the man," Joseph said with pride. "I loved him. He deserved better."

"Better than what?"

"He deserved better than to have been beaten, tortured, ridiculed and hung on a cross to die an agonizing death. This was to be my final resting place, but when Jesus was put to death I asked to be given his body to bury here."

As the man spoke I could read the conviction in his entire demeanour. His eyes locked onto mine intently, and he stood squarely facing me, his hands barely moving. It had been my experience with Hebrews that when they spoke they gestured constantly. All this led me to believe the man was intent on stressing his sincerity and the issue was very personal.

"What is *your* story?" I asked the Pharisee named Nicodemus.

"Both Joseph and I knew Jesus," he began. "We had the privilege to hear him speak. We believed what he taught. You must understand, Tribune, because of our positions in the community we could not openly follow him, but did so in secret."

"You are members of the Sanhedrin," I stated, and both of them nodded. "Your tribunal helped condemn the man. How do you explain that?"

"The Sanhedrin is made up of a seventy-one-man committee," Joseph told me. "Neither Nicodemus nor I agreed or consented to any action against Jesus."

"But you did not do anything to stop them," I said not at all certain it was true.

"You do not understand!" Joseph stated emphatically, but I suspected he was trying to convince himself. "There was nothing we could do to save him!"

The man appeared extremely anxious and his companion placed a reassuring hand on Joseph's shoulder.

"We are not proud of our actions, Tribune," Nicodemus uttered in a calm voice. It was the first time I had every seen Pharisee and Sadducee agree on any-thing. "We were outnumbered. Joseph spoke the truth—there was nothing we could do."

"So you sold your guilt for a hole in a rock," I remarked unsympathetically.

They looked at me shamefacedly and I knew their remorse to be genuine.

"Whom did you approach for permission to take the body?" I asked in a friendlier tone.

"Why, the Governor, of course," stated Joseph.

"Pilate," I said under my breath. "Then what did you do?"

It was Nicodemus who spoke: "Once we had his body I brought a mixture of aloes, myrrh and other aromatic plants and we wrapped them with his body in linen, as is our custom."

I nodded in understanding. That was what I had smelled in the tomb.

"We laid the body there," Joseph said stooping and pointing to a small ledge of rock inside the cave. "Then we rolled this stone in front of the entrance." He laid his hand on a large, round stone.

I studied the rock. It sat by the opening of the cave, and stood not quite as tall as a man. The rock was flat on two sides and its edge cut perfectly round. Like the inside of the tomb, the stone was whitewashed. A groove had been dug at the mouth of the cave so the rock could be rolled in place to block the opening. I stood beside the stone and attempted to move it. It did not budge. I put my shoulder to it and tried with all my might until finally it moved.

"You two could not have rolled this stone over the opening," I said breathing heavy from my exertions.

"Not the two of us alone," Joseph admitted. "Others were here."

"What others?"

"His followers; men mostly, but there were even some women."

"Women. Was Mary Magdalene among them?"

"Yes, she was."

"Then what happened?"

"I returned here later that evening," Joseph said.

"You did? Why?"

"I do not know exactly," he said. "I suppose I wished to be near him."

"Was anyone else here when you came?"

"Yes, there was. When I approached, I saw Roman guards in front of the tomb."

"What were they doing here?"

"They were doing nothing, simply standing around. I did not wish to be seen by them, so I left. I did not return until early yesterday morning. The guards were gone. No one was here. I was shocked to find the stone rolled away and the tomb empty."

"What did you do then?"

"I did not know what to do, so I went home and thought what I should do next. This morning I rushed off to find Nicodemus. I told him what I saw. He did not believe me, so I brought him here to see for himself."

I looked at Nicodemus who verified this with a nodding of his head.

"You said there were others here at the time of the burial." They nodded. "One or more of them may have returned after the burial, but before the guards arrived, and removed the body."

"For what purpose?" Nicodemus asked.

I decided not to answer. I thought a moment and said, more to myself than to them: "The stone may have been rolled away from the inside."

Both men regarded me with strange looks, and one of them said with some confusion: "We do not understand your meaning."

"Someone inside the tomb could have rolled away the stone."

"But the man was dead."

"Was he?" It was a question that had just occurred to me, but I did not wish to pursue it at this time. "What if someone stayed behind inside the tomb when you sealed it?"

"For what purpose?"

"Never mind the purpose," I said. "Was it possible that someone stayed inside and later rolled away the stone from inside the cave?"

"No," Joseph said simply.

"Why not?" I asked irritably. I was forming a viable theory, something that might occur to one in a thousand men, and I did not like having it quashed by an old Hebrew. "Might not someone have rolled away the stone from inside?"

"The rock is held in place by these wedges," Joseph spoke, and he stooped down and picked up two stones. "Once the rock is before the opening, these wedges are braced against it to keep the stone in place."

"So I see," I muttered, but had no intention of giving up on my theory. "Let us try a small test, shall we. I will go inside the tomb. The three of us will roll the rock in place. You two will secure it with the wedges and I shall attempt to remove the wedges and roll back the stone."

The two men regarded me as if I had suddenly gone mad. I assured them I had not, but it still took a bit of convincing to get them to comply.

From the outside the three of us moved the rock just enough so I might still slip inside the tomb. After I had done so, it was a little more difficult to roll the rock into place so it would completely cover the opening. I could no longer get a firm grip upon the rock, and my two assistants were not exactly up to the task physically. Persistence and encouragement on my part finally won out as the rock moved little by little until it was in place. I was amazed at how well it covered the entrance. Very little light came through the cracks, and I found I had to shout to be heard by Joseph and Nicodemus.

"Now place the wedges against the stone as you did originally," I instructed them. After a moment they called to me that they had done so. The absence of light forced me to feel around the rock to find the edge near the ground. Finding it, I attempted to slip my hand between the stone and the cave to reach the wedges. Since the rock fit so tightly against the cave and was bigger than the opening, I found I could not get even a finger to the outside. Thus I discovered my theory was flawed. A difficult thing for a Roman to admit.

"I cannot do it," I called out to my companions. There was no reply. "Remove the wedges and let us roll back the rock." Still no reply. In an instant I realized what a dangerous position I had placed myself in. I barely knew these men, and here I had aided them in sealing me up inside a tomb. Suddenly the air felt as if it had gone very thin. The walls, which I could see better now that my eyes had adjusted to the dark, seemed to be closing in on me. I could smell the sweet, sickening stenches of burial plants. They began to choke me. My breath came quick and shallow. A thin layer of cold sweat broke out over my entire body.

"Let us move aside the rock!" I cried out, trying not to sound frantic. Clutching hold of the stone I sought a firm purchase and attempted to roll it back. Fear and panic lent me strength and I strained against the rock. I braced my legs and back and summed up every ounce of strength to move the rock *manibus pedibusque*. My breathing became loud and laboured between the heavy grunts that coincided with my exertions. Finally I sensed the stone move. With that, I renewed my efforts, and a slow steady motioned followed. Sunlight broke into the tomb. Fresh air filled my lungs. I was barely aware of Joseph and Nicodemus pushing on the rock. When the opening was big enough, I forced my way out, scraping the skin of my arms and legs against the stone and the cave mouth. I practically fell to the ground, but the two older men were there to support me.

"Are you hurt, Tribune?" Nicodemus asked earnestly.

Out of breath I shook my head. "What happened?" I finally managed to say.

"We are no longer strong young men, Tribune," Joseph said through his heavy breathing. "We had exerted ourselves putting the stone in place. We found it difficult work to move it back again."

I regarded them closely looking for some sign of deception. I privately rebuked myself for thinking so evil of these two men.

With my hand I wiped the sweat from my forehead and face. I said: "For a moment I thought…"

"You thought what, Tribune?"

"Nothing. It is not important. Tell no one what transpired here," I instructed them.

"Tell no one of what?" they asked.

"Tell no one of anything. Tell no one of the empty tomb or our talk here. Now go your way. Hail Caesar!"

I added the last part to sound more official.

CHAPTER IV

▼

I waited at the tomb until Joseph of Arimathea and Nicodemus the Pharisee walked off out of sight. They would remain silent—about everything. I was convinced that they had nothing to do with the missing body, nor did they know who was behind its disappearance. I was curious, though, that Roman guards were stationed outside the tomb. Perhaps an inquiry in that direction was warranted.

If the Roman army was known for anything, it was its strict adherence to chain of command. It was this very thing that allowed one to trace back any detail to its commander. I began with a high ranked official, but was not received warmly. My reputation around the garrison was not a very good one because of what had occurred in Rome. It is curious how one's past can follow you, even halfway around the world. Even if some did not know the exact details that led up to my banishment, rumours about the Fortress were many. One rumour was that I had cursed the gods and defiled a temple. Another stated that I had cursed the Emperor and defiled his mistress. One rumour that was quite popular with the men from the Fortress was that while leading a cohort into battle, I had turned coward and fled the field leaving my men to be slaughtered. I cannot say I truly objected to any of these stories. None of them was as bad as the truth.

Eventually I was directed from commander to commander until I found a centurion by the name of Lucius Drusus. The centurion was a few years older than I, a little taller, a little broader. A strong jaw, heavy dark brows and a crooked nose all told me he was a formidable man, and one not to be crossed lightly. He reminded me of an ox with hay wrapped around its horn as a warning that the animal was given to goring. I found Drusus atop the northeast tower of the Antonia Fortress.

"What is it you want, Tribune?" he asked gruffly.

"My name of Claudius Maximus and—"

"I know who you are, Tribune. What is it you want?"

"I need honest answers to some honest questions," I said looking him straight in the eye. I figured it was an approach a man like he would accept.

"How about if I throw you off this tower instead," he said seriously. And I believed he meant it. He had hay on his horn, right enough.

Casually I looked over the edge of the tower. It was a long drop. Down there I could see trees and shrubs dotting a small valley. There were two large pools of water, but each was too far to break my fall. Beyond that I could see hills lined with olive groves. I glanced back at the centurion. There was a very slim chance that I could physically force him to cooperate, so I decided to use another approach.

"How about if you answer my questions first, and then you throw me off the tower?" I commented.

The man almost smiled. "That sounds reasonable," he said.

"May we go inside, away from the heat?" I requested. It was about midday, and the sun beat down mercilessly. I did not think I would ever get use to this climate.

Without saying a word he led me away, and we began the slow descent down the long flight of stairs I had just ascended to see him. It felt good to be out from under the sun.

"I understand you ordered some of your men to guard the tomb of a crucified man named Jesus." He nodded hesitantly. "Why?" I asked.

The centurion studied me closely as if trying to judge my motives. "Orders were given to me," he said. He spoke slowly choosing every word carefully.

"Orders from whom?"

He ceased his descent and took one step towards me. "Tribune, do you recall what we were told as young recruits? *Redime te captum quam queas minimo.*"

The centurion recited the prescription for soldierly conduct following capture by enemy troops, which loosely translated into; give the enemy as little help as possible.

I stopped short on the step above him that brought me up to his height. I faced him. He was an intimidating figure. I could not force answers out of the man, but I had to show him I was not willing to climb down from my chariot.

"Centurion," I began, "we are not enemies." My voice was friendly but firm. "We are both on the same side. We are both loyal to Rome. We belong to a royal brotherhood."

"We are not brothers," he remarked as he continued his descent. "Your loyalty to Rome is not beyond reproach, and the last centurion who answered questions from a tribune, is now patrolling the middle of the Judean Wilderness. I tell you what you want, and the next thing I know, I'm being dressed down for something I didn't even do."

"Could you simply give me the names of the men who stood guard outside the tomb the other day?"

"No."

I saw that it was not progressing the way I had hoped.

"Centurion, I am only trying simply to do my duty," I told him.

"What duty?"

"I am looking into why the body of the Nazarene, Jesus, is missing from his tomb," I said bluntly.

The words appeared to have a most profound effect upon the man. We had reached the bottom of the stairs and he simply stood there leaning against the wall, with his jaw slack and his deep-set eyes staring past me, focussing on nothing in particular.

"What is it, Centurion?" I asked perplexed.

He turned away from me clenching and unclenching his two mighty hands. He began to walk slowly until we came to a small, dingy courtyard where very little sunlight shined in. Stone benches lined the sides and a stone pillar stood upright in the middle of the floor.

"I knew him," Drusus spoke more softly than I ever imagined he could speak.

"Who?"

"The man named Jesus. The other day he was brought before Pilate and he became my charge. He was my prisoner, but he was the most compliant prisoner I had ever seen. He gave us no trouble. When he was condemned to die, he was treated the same as any condemned man—no better, no worse."

I studied the centurion as he spoke. I had never seen such a quick change in a man's manner. What was he trying to hide, I thought—guilt? remorse? It grew more obvious as he spoke.

"When it was determined he was going to die, we stripped him and bound him to a post. I ordered my men to flog him." Drusus laid his right hand gently upon the stone pillar, and I realized that this was where it had taken place. Perhaps that was the Nazarene's blood dotting the stones. "I ordered forty lashes."

He looked around briefly and spotted a short leather whip that hung upon the wall. He walked over to the wall, removed the whip and examined it closely.

"Have you ever used a *flagrum* on a man, Tribune," he said. "They have small lead balls and bits of sharp bone in them, so that when you use it to whip a man, it tears at his flesh. It was used on the man Jesus. The man was bleeding badly. He had taken thirty-nine lashes, but I could not bear to see him take even one more, so I stopped the scourging. Do not ask me why I did. I simply did. My men protested that I was cheating the prisoner his due punishment. I gave them a look that if they said one more word I would crush their skulls, and they backed down. We untied the prisoner from the post and he fell to the ground weak and trembling with pain. It was said that the man claimed he was some kind of Hebrew king, and as a cruel jest one of my men wove a thorny crown from the branches of a jujube tree and thrust it on his head. Another of them put a scarlet robe over him, then they mocked him, and spat on him. I wanted to stop them, but I did not."

Drusus spoke as if he were under a spell. I was not certain, but I believed tears welled in his eyes as he told his story. It was curious.

"Why all the sympathy?" I wanted to know.

He turned to me, still in a half daze. "I am not sure," he replied and continued his report. "We brought him back before the Governor. For some reason I hoped Pilate would have pity on the man after his beating, and release him—but that was not to be. Pilate displayed Jesus before the crowd that gathered and said to them, 'Behold the man.' I believe the Governor thought this display would be enough, but the crowd cried for the man's death. Pilate washed his hands of the affair and condemned the man.

"The prisoner was given back his own clothes, and forced to carry a *patibulum* through the streets. He was so weak I did not see how he would make it. He stumbled as he made his way along. After he fell down two or three times I picked a man out of the throng that lined the streets, and had him carry the cross-piece. It was not that far a walk to Calvary, but it seemed to take longer than it did. The majority of the crowds seemed to enjoy the drama. Some jeered him and ridiculed him. Some women wept for him." Here again I could see the remorse in the centurion's face as he recalled the event. "At one point a woman came forward to wipe the blood and sweat from his face. Jesus said something to her, but I could not hear it. We reached the summit of Calvary where he was stripped of his clothes and knocked to the ground. I had my men stretch out his arms across the *patibulum* and spikes were driven through his wrists into the wood. The crosspiece was set onto the *stipes* and his feet were nailed to *suppedaneum*. It was about the third hour of the day. Above his head the Governor ordered us to hang the *titulus*: JESUS OF NAZARETH, THE KING OF THE JEWS. I think it was Pilate's idea of a jest."

The centurion forced a grin but there was no mirth in it. "Have you ever witnessed a crucifixion, Tribune?" he asked. I did not answer. "It is not a pretty scene. The suffering is indescribable. The sheer agony can be seen in every twitching muscle, and in the twisted features of the victim's face, and the haunting moans that go on and on and on. Sometimes, I swear, I can hear those moans even after they're dead. How is that possible?" The centurion turned to me in askance, but his deep-set eyes seemed to look through me. I spoke the centurion's name to help bring him out of whatever spell he was under. Drusus focussed in on my face and continued. "His own people mocked him as he hung there, but some who knew him were there to grieve, and they kept watch hour after hour. Two other men were crucified along with him, one on each side. They exchanged words, but I could not make out what they said. It appeared that even amid all his suffering Jesus was trying to comfort them, for he spoke to them gently. Perhaps they knew each another, I do not know.

"After a time my men grew bored and restless. They decided to cast lots, but with nothing to wager they picked up the Nazarene's garment and gambled for it. Nothing much happened until about the sixth hour. The sky grew dark and I expected it was the coming of a storm, but not like any storm I had ever seen. A woman approached the cross with a young man. Someone told me this was the mother of Jesus. She looked quite humble, and almost..." The centurion did not finish, but added: "Her grief must have been powerful. At the ninth hour I suspected the end was near for him. I had seen men last longer on the cross, but he did not seem strong. He cried out for a drink. I had one of my men soak a sponge in wine, and sticking the sponge on the end of a spear he offered it up to the dying man. He said something else and then he died." Drusus shook his head with a look of wonder.

"What is it?" I prompted him.

"You may think this strange, Tribune, but the moment he gave up the ghost, the earth shook. Never before was I ashamed of doing my duty, but I was ashamed that day, for I knew that he had been a righteous man."

"Why do you say that?"

"I just know," responded Drusus. "Even as he was *in articulo mortis*, in the grasp of death, he asked his God to forgive us—us, the very ones who persecuted him." Drusus fell silent.

After a considerable bout of silence I asked: "What happened then?"

Drusus continued to stare off, and at first I thought he hadn't heard me. Then he looked up at me and spoke.

"Some locals arrived at the scene. They wanted the bodies brought down and buried before nightfall—something to do with their beliefs. I knew that the two on either side of the Nazarene were still alive. They were supporting themselves with their legs against the *suppedaneum*, and by doing so they were prolonging their end. I ordered their legs be broken below the knees. That way, without their legs to support them, they would hang only by the wrists, which brings death all the quicker. But when my man approached the centre cross I stopped him from breaking the legs of Jesus. 'He is dead', I told them. They all turned to me as if I were spoiling their fun. 'He is dead!' I repeated. They all backed away except a soldier named Marius, who is tough by nature and cruel by choice. Marius snatched up a spear and said: 'One way to know for certain.' And he drove the spear into the side of Jesus. I could have clouted the man on the head."

"Then what occurred?"

"Shortly after I was called to appear before Pontius Pilate. The Prefect wished to know if Jesus was dead."

"Does the Governor always take such an interest in prisoners who are crucified?" I asked.

The big man shrugged his shoulders and shook his head. "I do not know why the Prefect showed interest in this man, but I told him the man was dead."

"What occurred next?"

"The three bodies were taken down from their crosses and removed."

"And you do not know what happened to the body of Jesus after that?"

"No, but my men should know."

"How would they know?"

"For some reason soldiers were ordered to guard the burial tomb of Jesus. It was not desirable duty, but I was not pleased with their conduct, so I sent them."

"The same men who tortured Jesus were sent to guard his body," I said, marvelling at life's little jests. "Who ordered the guards for the tomb?"

"The Governor."

"Strange," I commented, then asked: "Where might I find these soldiers who guarded the tomb?"

"They are out on patrol at this time, but should be back in the fortress before nightfall." At my request Lucius Drusus described the men so I might know them by sight. Though I did not ask, the centurion also gave me what details he knew of these men.

"I have only one question remaining," I said. "Can you say for certain, beyond all doubt, that when the body of Jesus was taken down from the cross, he was dead?"

I read a trace of uncertainty on the centurion's face, and I believed I was on to something.

His head began to nod. "Yes," he spoke. "I am certain he was quite dead."

My crestfallen face must have betrayed my disappointment. It was a theory I had grown fond of, and was not ready to totally give up. "You are absolutely certain: there was not a spark of life left in the man."

"I am quite certain," Drusus said, but I did not believe him.

"Thank you, Centurion. You have been helpful."

I turned to leave but had not gone far when Drusus called out to me.

"Tribune, there is one other thing I must tell you. I do not know if it means anything."

"Yes?"

"When Marius thrust his spear into the side of the Nazarene, blood came forth."

Somehow I knew there was more.

"Blood came forth, and so did water."

"Water?" I repeated, perplexed. "Have you ever heard of such a thing?"

"No, Tribune. Never."

"What could it mean?" I asked.

He shrugged his heavy broad shoulders and said no more.

CHAPTER V

▼

I had a considerable amount of time before the soldiers I wished to question returned to the Fortress. I decided to make good use of it.

Passing through the northwest gate, I walked south outside the western wall of the city. Here, lined up side-by-side, packed tightly together were stalls of merchants, farmers, and peddlers hawking their wares to residents and pilgrims alike. In the bazaar could be found anything and everything: fruits and vegetables, spices and perfumes, garments and fabrics, glassware, copperware, pottery and brass.

The market was a great place of learning. Lesson one: never accept anyone's first offer. Prices were purposely inflated strictly for the intention of haggling. Personally, I did not see why the merchants could not simply ask an honest price, but these people had strange ways. Lesson two: if someone claims the item is solid gold, bite down on it first. In the bazaar things were seldom what they seemed. Lesson three: hold onto your purse or someone might mistake it for their own.

This late in the afternoon trading did not seem as intense as earlier in the day, but the bazaar was just as crowded. The populace was drawn here. The market was a daily social event where greetings were exchanged and one could pick up on the latest news and gossip—at least three different versions. The bazaar also attracted an undesirable class such as thieves and beggars, and some beggars who were thieves.

I walked along eating a pressed cake of dried fruit until I came to the next gate. At the gate there sat a pitiable creature as one is likely to see in all Judea. He was dressed in old, filthy clothes, and worn sandals. A dirty rag was tied around his head covering his eyes. He sat cross-legged on a worn mat, and held an old wooden bowl in both his hands. Of all the beggars in Jerusalem, Blind Man's bowl was the biggest.

"Alms," he cried out in a cracked and mournful voice. "Alms for the poor, the blind, the aged. Alms."

"Is business good, Blind Man?" I asked standing over him.

"Alms," he repeated.

I nodded my head, reached into my purse, removed a few small coins and dropped them into his bowl. The sound caused him to smile a wide, toothless grin that did nothing to enhance his features.

"Business is good, life is sweet and God is merciful!" he spoke. "And how are you, Tribune Maximus?"

I ignored the amenities and came directly to the point. "I need some information," I told him. Blind Man was one of my more reliable sources in Jerusalem. I could always trust him to know what was going on in the city. He had the uncanny ability to hear and see all that occurred in Jerusalem. I was one of the few people in the city who knew Blind Man was not truly blind, but a professional beggar who feigned sightlessness to garner sympathy and money. He was good at gathering information, for most people will do things and say things in front of a blind man that they might not normally do with anyone else.

I stood to one side of him and cast casual glances around attempting to look inconspicuous. "What do you hear, Blind Man?" I asked speaking out the side of my mouth.

"I hear everything," he said in a low voice, barely moving his lips. "What do you want to know?"

"I am looking into the disappearance of Jesus of Nazareth."

"I heard he was dead."

"And so he is, but his body is missing from his tomb."

"That is something you don't hear every day."

"Are you saying you know nothing regarding it?"

"I didn't say that."

"Then you do know something."

"I didn't say that either."

"Tell me what you know."

"Alms! Alms for the poor, the blind, the aged," he called out.

I took a few more coins from my purse and dropped them into his bowl.

"Not only is this Jesus missing from his tomb, but he's been seen walking about," Blind Man told me in a low voice.

"Have you seen him?"

"No. But there are rumours that he is not truly dead."

"He's dead. I just spoke with a man who swears he died on the cross. Someone might be pretending to be him."

"Perhaps."

"What can you tell me about his followers?"

"He had twelve who were devoted to him while he lived. All of them were Galileans."

"Where can I find them?"

"If they were wise, they returned to Galilee."

"Find out if they are still in Jerusalem. Also, a woman named Mary Magdalene."

"If they are in Jerusalem, I will find them."

"Make it fast, Blind Man, I need to speak with them."

"Yes, noble Tribune," he spoke in a loud voice. "Thank you, noble Tribune."

"Cut the crap," I muttered and walked away.

CHAPTER VI

▼

Back at Antonia Fortress I waited in the barracks for the tomb guards to return from their patrol so I might interrogate them. When a crowd of soldiers entered the quarters, I recognized the guards in question from the descriptions their commander, Lucius Drusus, had given me. I followed them to their billets, so I could observe them closely. Flavius was the youngest. He was tall and slim with delicate features. He seemed to be a quiet youth, and I instinctually knew that if it came down to it, he would be a good source of information—he was breakable. Two of the others were Titus and Scarus. It was difficult to say which one was more dull-witted. Titus was short and stocky with a thick neck upon which rested an even thicker head. Scarus was taller but about as broad. Both had thick, dark hair, large noses, and heavy brows beneath sloping foreheads. They may not have had a brain between them, but they could prove dangerous if backed into a corner. The one to watch carefully was Marius. Lucius Drusus warned me about him. As soon as I saw him, I knew his ilk, *miles gloriosus*—a boastful soldier. Perhaps he had a reason to boast. Marius was tall, muscular, intelligent looking and brave. Drusus had also mentioned something else about him—Marius was cruel. I had heard the story that circulated about the Fortress regarding Marius. Just before my arrival in Jerusalem, Marius had been a centurion. One day, in a fit of rage, he killed a subordinate with his bare hands. Marius was duly reduced in rank with no hope of ever getting it back. Out of habit some stilled referred to him as 'centurion'. Others in the Legion called him that out of ridicule—but never to his face. There was a malevolence about him. It hung on him like an evil charm around his neck. I could see it in his eyes, and in the way the right side of his mouth curled up into a tight-lip grin. He kept his hair cropped short, and like all good Romans, and his companions, Marius was clean shaven.

They were in the dress of a soldier of the legion, a trifle dusty from their patrol, carrying a javelin, and shield. On their head each wore an iron helmet and on their feet heavy, thick sandals studded with hobnails. Their tunics were dull-red of heavy wool worn beneath mail armour tied with a military belt. In the front of the belt hung a dangling apron of long studded leather straps. A sword, with its long tapering point, hung on the right side, while a dagger was worn on the left.

"I am Tribune Maximus," I stated. "I need to ask you men some questions." Each was heavily armed and regarded me hostilely, but I knew my rank would protect me—for the time being.

"I understand you men were present at the crucifixion of three Jews last Friday," I said.

Marius took a step towards me. "That's true," he said speaking for the group.

"Did anything strange occur during the crucifixion?"

All four exchanged curious looks, turned to Marius, then back to me with shrugs and blank stares.

"Nothing strange," Marius spoke. "Just another crucifixion. Three fewer Jews to worry about. What causes you to think anything strange occurred?"

"I was speaking with your commander, Drusus, and he said—"

Marius laughed heartily, and the others followed, but their laughter sounded nervous and awkward.

"Drusus is the one who's been acting strangely," Marius commented. "I believe that last crucifixion disturbed him."

"Why do you say that?" I asked.

Marius shrugged. "His heart just didn't seem in it."

"I think he felt sorry for the Nazarene," Titus spoke up.

"He told us to go easy on him," Scarus added.

"A crown of thorns and forty lashes does not sound easy to me," I remarked.

Marius's face changed from amicable to hateful in a blink. This man's temper was as short as his hair. "It was only thirty-nine lashes," he uttered while his eyes smouldered.

"We were only doing our duty," said Scarus.

"We've given others far worse," added Titus. "Drusus made us go easy on him."

"Why was that?" I asked, but only received more shrugs and blank stares.

"Maybe Drusus is getting soft in his old age," responded Marius sarcastically.

"When I spoke with Drusus he threatened to throw me off the roof of the tower," I told them.

"A week ago he would have done it," Titus remarked in earnest.

"Maybe Drusus believes what others are saying about the Nazarene," Scarus said.

"What are they saying?" I asked.

"That he was the messiah, come to save the Jews."

"Drusus thought he was a righteous man," I stated.

"Is that what he told you?" Marius asked me. I nodded and he said: "I was standing as close to Drusus as I am to you. When the Jew died, the centurion looked up at him and said, 'Truly this was the Son of God.' Now, what do you think of that, Tribune?"

"You don't believe he was?" I asked Marius.

He snorted a reply, and said: "Let the Jews believe what they will; I'll put my faith in my sword."

"He did have a following," I added.

Marius snorted again—it must have been a favourite expression of his. "We saw his following," he mentioned with disgust. "A fainthearted bunch if ever there was one. It was one of his own men who betrayed him."

"How do you know?"

"We witnessed it ourselves," spoke Titus. "We were ordered to arrest the man, Jesus, and bring him to the Jewish authorities for questioning."

"Who ordered it?"

"Pontius Pilate himself ordered it," announced Scarus with pride.

"Tell me what occurred."

Marius gave his companions a cursory glance, then turned and faced me boldly. "We were ordered to accompany some Temple guards to arrest the man Jesus and bring him before Caiaphas, the high priest. A group of priests and elders joined us, and among that group was one of Jesus's own men, Judas Iscariot, whose job it was to point out the man. We heard tell that the Jewish high priest paid Iscariot thirty pieces of silver to betray Jesus."

My entire body stiffened involuntarily, and I hoped none of them noticed. I motioned for Marius to continue.

"It was late, and some carried torches for light. Along the way we seemed to attract more people until our number grew quite large. Iscariot told us we would find Jesus in a garden outside the east wall of the city. He led us to a spot where some men were standing about. Iscariot came forward, greeted the man and kissed him. That was his signal. We stepped up and took the man."

"Jesus put up no resistance?" I queried. They all shook their heads. "And his companions simply allowed you to take him?"

"I told you, they were a fainthearted bunch," Marius said. "They all turned and fled. I attempted to stop one of them. I grabbed at his robe and it came off in my hands. The coward ran off *in naturalibus*."

The four of them laughed at this recollection.

"What did you do with Jesus?"

"It was a busy night," Marius uttered. "He was brought before the Jewish high priest, then to the Prefect, the tetrarch Herod, then back to Pilate for sentencing. We did not get any sleep that night."

"Nor the following day, I gather," said I. "You men were in charge of the prisoner the day of the crucifixion, and were ordered to guard his tomb afterwards."

All of them became quiet and still. They appeared uneasy that I knew so much regarding their past duties.

"That is correct, Tribune," Marius admitted somewhat reluctantly.

"You men were ordered to guard the tomb, and now the body is missing," I commented. "That will not reflect well on your service record." This comment only garnered me more hostile glares.

"We've been disciplined, Tribune," Scarus spoke through gritted teeth.

"And we certainly don't need you to remind us how we failed in our duty," Marius added.

"Perhaps you can tell me exactly what occurred at the tomb," I spoke looking directly at Marius, who continued to stare back at me mutely. His silence was a clear challenge of my authority, so I decided to use it. "You will either answer my questions here and now, or I will take you somewhere less pleasant."

"Tribune, are you threatening me?" he said grinning almost savagely. Obviously Marius was well versed at putting on a show of strength in front of his companions. Prudence dictated that I not challenge him physically, even if he did not have three men behind him.

"You know," Marius spoke to his companions without taking his eyes off me, "I heard of a tribune named Maximus. It is said this tribune cannot return to Rome, and that even his own family has renounced him—what's left of them, anyway."

I took a step towards Marius, and looking him in the eyes I uttered: "Do not ever mention my family again, Centurion." Then in a mocking tone I added: "No, that is not correct. You are not a centurion. Not any longer."

Marius's continence stiffened and his eyes smouldered, but he said nothing.

"Now Marius, you will answer my questions," I told him, allowing some of my own ire to rise. "It is an authority appointed to me by the Emperor."

"It was the Emperor who banished you."

"But he did not strip me of my rank," I informed him. "What I do is the will of the Praetor of Jerusalem, and more than that, the will of the Emperor himself. What I do is in the name of Caesar. Whom do *you* serve?"

This was enough to bring the man back to right-thinking.

"As we said, it had been a long day," Marius began. "None of us had slept for a day and a night. We looked on it as easy duty—guard a dead man's tomb. I think Drusus was trying to punish us. We slept in shifts, but by the second day we grew bored and though it was not allowed I procured a goatskin of wine that we passed around. We must have all fallen asleep, for when we woke we discovered the stone had been rolled away, and the tomb empty."

"This all occurred the morning of *dies solis*?"

"Yes, Tribune. His followers must have been watching us closely, and when we fell asleep, they crept in and stole the body."

"For what purpose?" I asked.

"Who knows why Jews do anything?" Titus spoke up.

"They have all sorts of strange rites and practices," Scarus added.

I turned to young Flavius who had been conspicuously quiet the entire time.

"And what do you have to say?" I asked him directly.

He remained silent for a moment then spoke: "Exactly what my comrades told you, Tribune; we fell asleep and they took the body."

He spoke it in the manner of an unconvincing litany—rehearsed but not truthful. I did not know what they were hiding but I intended to find out—eventually.

"Sleeping on guard duty is a very serious offence," I stated and asked them: "What did Lucius Drusus say about it?"

"He raised Hades over it," Marius admitted with a wry grin. "The Centurion dressed us down, but to me, he did not appear that concerned."

"As if he knew it was going to happen?" I muttered. "Did any of you recall seeing Drusus after the crucifixion?" They all looked at one another and shook their heads.

"I don't believe we understand your meaning, Tribune," said Marius.

I shrugged and did not answer. "Do you know where I can find the disciples of Jesus? I believe there were twelve of them."

It was their turn to shrug.

"Might you know where I can find the woman Mary Magdalene?"

Titus and Scarus both laughed, and one of them said: "Looking to get some, Tribune?"

But I was watching Marius who said: "Don't know, Tribune."

"You don't know much, do you?" I remarked.

Marius looked at me as if he wished to kill me and said: "I know what I need to know."

I took his meaning and asked: "One last question; are you certain the Nazarene was dead when he was taken down from the cross?"

They all looked at me as if it were the most ridiculous question they had ever heard, but then their faces took on a hint of uncertainty

"He was dead," Marius spoke up boldly.

"How can you be certain?"

Marius snatched up his spear and poised it at me threateningly.

"Because I put this in his side just to be sure."

It was a blatant threat. Marius wanted me to know that the next time we met alone, one of us would die.

I gave a curt salute and took my leave.

CHAPTER VII

▼

Expectations are a strange thing. A man may start out with great expectations for his life—power, fame, respect of his countrymen, love of his family—and yet he may never achieve any of them. At one time I expected all those things for my life. They were awards to be sought after, fought over, sacrificed for, pursued and gained. I had done all that, and in turn achieved each one. And once I had them, had them in the palm of my hand, I lost them all in an instant. Expectations will do that to you. Take this assignment for example: I expected it would be simple and short, over in a day. Unfortunately, the more questions I asked, the more questions were raised. The more people I talked to, the more people I had to talk to. The sun was going down over Jerusalem and I felt more behind in a solution than when I had started.

I searched for Blind Man to see if he had learned anything regarding Jesus's followers. I knew it was too soon, but I looked regardless. It appeared Blind Man was nowhere to be found, so I left my name with all the right people in hopes that it would reach him.

I continued to walk the streets mulling over in my mind the problem of this missing messiah and the variety of suspicious characters I had met, and some I had not. The followers of Jesus were still first on my list for stealing the body of their friend. Where they were, remained a mystery, but I was certain that if I found them, I would find the body. Joseph of Arimathea and Nicodemus appeared innocent, but it did seem convenient that Joseph just happened to have a tomb to use when the need arose. Then again, the two of them could have left me in that cave to die. What was disturbing Lucius Drusus so? I was certain the four Roman soldiers I had just spoken with were not telling me the truth. What could have happened at the tomb that they should have to lie? It had to be something worse than drinking and falling asleep on duty. And if so, what could it possibly be?

It was all too confusing. It was all too much for my tired mind to unravel. I decided to rest and relax and reward myself with some very cheap wine in an establishment I was particularly fond of, though it was not particularly fond of me. It was my own fallibility, for you see, I did have a tendency to be quite obnoxious when in my cups. It was late when I arrived there, and I can only assume it was quite late when I was requested or forced to leave. I do remember that I emptied my purse and got what I could on credit. I do not remember being thrown out, so I must have left on good terms with the owner and patrons alike.

Navigating home did prove a bit of a problem along the dark, narrow and uneven streets of Jerusalem. I suppose I had been drunker, but not much. The ground seemed to be moving beneath my feet, and I began to question my whereabouts. There was a sound behind me, and I swore someone called to me in Aramaic, the street language of the natives. I turned in time to have something hard hit me between the eyes. Jupiter! Everything went black and tiny flashing stars danced before me. I staggered backward, and hit the ground hard. Before I could sit up, bodies swarmed over me striking and kicking me viciously. They cursed me in Aramaic, and uttered 'Don't try to find our messiah!', and 'Forget about him who was in the tomb!'. I was surprised that these Hebrews could deliver their message so forcefully. It was a good pummelling. I don't think I every received better. The beating seemed to go on and on, and I hoped I would pass out before long, but my thick skull allowed me to remain conscious. Try as I might I could not fight back, though at one time my hand went up under the long garment of one of my assailants and I grabbed hold of something. I thought it might be his privates, so I yanked as hard as I could, and that something came off in my hand. If it was his privates, he would be in considerably more discomfort than me. The beating continued, and soon I felt myself begin to pass out as a black cloud enveloped me. Only vaguely do I remember coming back to consciousness, and crawling on my belly along the street. How I found my way back to my quarters is a mystery.

When my swollen eyes opened, they beheld a vision of loveliness bending over me. Her eyes were wide and reminded me of emeralds. They were beautiful, but held a hint of sadness that remained even when she smiled. The veil she wore on her head allowed some of her brown hair to show its thick, rich lustre. I often told her she looked like a Jewish princess, though I had never seen one. Her olive skin was smooth and soft to the touch, as were her full red lips that seldom smiled. Perhaps that was why I allowed Ruth to stay with me. I do not believe I could tolerate a cheerful person to be around me. I had chosen to be unhappy, and would only tolerate unhappy people in my life. We had met three months ago, and I had her move in almost immediately. I do not know what kept the two of us together; I never questioned it. How long we would stay together was something that did not concern me. We took from each other what we could, and that seemed enough, at least for me.

I lay there staring up at her as she gently treated my cuts and bruises with oils. Among her other talents, Ruth had a crude knowledge of working with *materia medica*. More times than I could count was she able to concoct some kind of remedy for me when I was ill or had come home in a similar condition. She would not look in my eyes. She said it was too painful when I was like this.

"What was it this time?" she asked tight-lipped, which meant she was not at all pleased with me. She said 'this time' as if this happened twice a week. Truth was, it only happened every second week.

I did not attempt to answer her, but made a move to sit up. She did not try to restrain me. I wish she had. A sudden and unpleasant rush to my head forced me to recline. Ruth stood up and took away the cloth and bowl, and the alabastrons of oil.

The room was partially lit and sparsely furnished. Ruth had sometimes said how the room reflected the man—simple and austere. Every time she said it I felt like I was being complimented and insulted at the same time. I do not think I would have taken that from anyone but Ruth.

She came and sat next to me in silence. When I felt I had waited long enough I told her everything. I told how I got my assignment, had gone to see Marcus Malachi, visited the tomb, and met Joseph and Nicodemus. I left out the part about allowing myself to be sealed up in the cave. I told her of my talk with the centurion, Lucius Drusus, and the four men under his command. I explained to her my thoughts on the case. Ruth listened. She always listened.

"It was your own countrymen who attacked me tonight," I told her with a modicum of resentment. "I did not think Jews could hit that hard."

Ruth did not comment.

"I sent Blind Man to find the followers of this man Jesus," I told her.

"Do you think he will find them?" she asked, in her soft, gentle voice. It was a voice that I thought would break if she ever raised it.

"If anyone can find them, Blind Man can."

"Is it important you find the body of Jesus?" she asked looking at me with her melancholic eyes.

"It is my duty," I stated simply. "What else have I except my duty?"

She winced as if struck and asked: "And when you have done your duty, will the Emperor allow you to return to Rome?"

I stared at her with a look of anger, fear and loathing all rolled into one. I do not know where these feelings originated, or why they were directed at Ruth, but they were.

"That is a decision for Tiberias," I told her sternly.

She knelt down at my feet and lay her head in my lap.

"One day," she said, "when you do return to Rome, I will miss you." I did not respond. "And on that day you return to Rome, will you miss me?" I did not respond.

I did not sleep well that night, but I slept.

The following morning I was stiff and sore but the swelling had gone down some.

"You should rest today," Ruth told me with her usual degree of concern.

"I know," was my response, "but I must see the Prefect today."

"You should not see him looking like that. It is not proper."

I looked myself over. Besides the bruises and scratches, I observed a plethora of small round dots marked the skin on parts of my body. Ruth told me there were also some on my face and back. The pattern looked familiar to me, though I could not remember where I had seen them.

CHAPTER VIII

▼

That morning Ruth insisted I visit the baths before my meeting with the Prefect. As I went from the *frigidarium* to the *tepidarium* to the steam-filled *calidarium*, I reviewed the events of the past day and prepared what I would say to Pontius Pilate. This would prove to be an important interview, and since the Governor held my future in his hands, I intended to tread softly. If I handled this matter just right, it might very well be my passage back to Rome.

Pontius Pilate had received his appointment from Emperor Tiberias, and took over the governorship of Judea about three years ago. I had only been in Judea a year. Pilate had a reputation as a good administrator. The construction of the new aqueduct had garnered him much praise from all quarters. Since Jerusalem was on the edge of a desert, everyone appreciated the need for water in the city. As an administrator, Pontius Pilate managed to exceed the usual amount of bribery, corruption, cruelty, murder, misappropriation of funds and malfeasance, while still carrying out his duties. For a Roman, duty was the main objective, and we carried it out *per fas et nefas*—through right and wrong. Pilate's position of governor gave him control of the military forces, and he carried the authority to order the death sentence. His feeling towards the Jews was no secret; he did not like them. The Jews, of course, reciprocated similarly. As Governor of Judea his home was in Caesarea, the Roman administrative centre. Fortunately for me, the Governor was still in Jerusalem. As it was, the Prefect would not see me until midday. While I waited, I privately thanked Ruth for convincing me to visit the baths before my interview with Pilate. I felt clean and refreshed, prepared for any eventuality.

I was shown into an audience chamber of Pontius Pilate's residence in Jerusalem. The room was richly decorated with ornately carved columns, and imitation marble panels on the wall. Several chairs and statues stood around the room. In the centre of the room was an ornamental pool whose bottom consisted of an intricate wave-pattern mosaic. To the right of the double doors I entered, were two long steps that ran half the length of the room to a balcony. Against the far wall, upon a handsome chair with eagle heads carved into the arms, and surrounded by attendants, sat the prefect.

Pontius Pilate was a serious looking man. He was tall and thin and bony. Bony shoulders poked through his toga. Bony elbows rested on the arms of his chair. And bony knees peeked out at me from beneath his tunic. His thin lips did not smile, for fear people would not take him seriously, and so he also refrained from revealing any humour or wit. His close-set blue eyes regarded me curtly. Pilate seldom looked at me directly during the interview, but chose, instead, to study his hands.

"Claudius Maximus, what happened to you?" he asked more out of curiosity than concern.

"An accident, your excellency" I responded.

He clearly did not like that answer. "It distresses us that one of our tribunes allows himself to be seen in public in this condition. I trust you will be more careful in the future."

"Yes, Prefect."

"What is it you wished to see us about?" His thin lips barely moved as he spoke. His voice and manner were condescending. This was not going to be at all pleasant.

"Prefect, I am tending to the matter of a disappearance of a body from its tomb." I regarded him closely for some sort of reaction, but he revealed none. "Do you recall the man? His name was Jesus. He was crucified last Friday. I was led to understand you were interested in the incident."

"Yes, Tribune," he exclaimed hastily. "You need not remind us. What is it you want?"

"I find I must know the details that led up to his crucifixion." Pilate sat and with a wave of his hand, his dismissed the attendants. The governor waited until they were out of the room before he allowed me to continue. "Prefect, I understand you presided over the trial, and pronounced sentence on him."

Still he said nothing. He was not going to make this at all easy for me. I decided to stare back. It worked. After a tense moment he spoke.

"When the man Jesus was brought before me, it was simply *pro forma*. His fate had already been determined by his own people, and in regards to them, they were merely going through political channels. It was all predicted."

"But Prefect, you have total authority," I spoke as politely as I could. "The man did not have to die."

Pontius Pilate did not appear to agree. He regarded me coldly, and then continued.

"The governorship of Judea is not an easy nor simple task," he began in a monotone voice. "For one thing I must keep Rome happy, and that means money in the way of taxes. It is also my duty to bring Roman law and Roman order to these desert people." He said 'desert people' with no little contempt. "These Jews are a thick-neck lot. You could fill parchment after parchment with their laws and customs. And they cling to these laws and customs as if their very lives depended on them. I, on the other hand, must impose Roman law while trying to keep these people from open rebellion. I am a military governor, yes, and I have the might of our legions under my command, but I am a governor never-the-less, which means I must carefully choose when to force the will of Rome upon the Hebrews, and when to gracefully withdraw from a situation where the possible consequence would outweigh any benefit. Before I came to Judea, the Emperor himself entrusted me with the *Pax Romana*—the peace of Rome. I intend to honour that trust.

"You were not present in Jerusalem at the time, Tribune, but one of my first acts after arriving here was to erect image-baring standards in the city. You would think that to be a very common, and simple decision. Not so when dealing with Jews. They considered the standards idolatrous. They petitioned me to remove the standards. I declined. The next thing I knew they protested vigorously, and finally I was forced to remove the standards. As Romans—as leaders of the world—we understand that these decisions must be made from time to time. Your father understood.

"If one man must die so Jerusalem may have a little peace, then clearly *exitus acta probat*—the result validates the deed. Is that so difficult to understand, Tribune? Besides, if it does not deal directly with Rome, or pose any threat to Rome I allow the Jews to handle their own affairs."

This I knew to be only partly true. Pilate himself could appoint the Jewish high priest, and he exercised control over funds in the Temple treasury. It was not common knowledge around Jerusalem, but I knew that Pilate was using Temple funds to help pay for the new aqueduct that brought water into the city from a nearby spring. I decided not to reveal to Pilate that I was privy to this information.

"Prefect, could you tell me something of the man Jesus?" I asked him.

Pilate stared off trying to make it appear he was not thinking about the question.

"He was a man like any other," he replied.

"Was he intelligent?"

"At times he appeared most intelligent," Pilate admitted. "Yet at other times he appeared quite ignorant and stupid."

"How so?"

"Even after being impressed with the severity of the matter, the man would not say a word in his own defence."

"Surely he could see the gravity of the situation," I suggested.

"I suspected he knew. He simply did not care."

"What did he say?"

"Very little. I asked him if he were the messiah, a self-proclaimed king of the Jews. He said these words were not his."

"Why did you ask him that?"

It was clear Pilate did not like being questioned.

"These were the accusations made by the high priests," he spoke slowly and deliberately.

"Were they present during the questioning?"

"No. They waited outside."

"Why was that?"

Pilate shook his head. "They made some reference about not being allowed inside the praetorium during their holiday. As I told you, they have a myriad of rules and laws."

"What happened then?"

"Jesus would say little else. I went out to the high priests to tell them I found no guilt in the man. They insisted he was a criminal. 'Then try him yourselves!' I told them in disgust. They make me sick, these so-called 'holy-men'.

"They practically told me they wanted the man dead, and I was the only one authorized to order the death sentence. I wanted no part of it, so I ordered the man to be brought before Herod."

"Why Herod?"

"Jesus was a Galilean. As tetrarch, Herod's domain encompasses Galilee."

"What did Herod do?"

"How should I know? He questioned the man and sent him back to me."

"Passing the *sestertius*," I observed.

"*Respondeat superior*! The *sestertius* stops here!" Pilate responded forcibly and with some anger, as he pointed to the floor in front of him. "Jesus was again brought before me and again I tried to save him."

"Why?" I asked. I knew Pilate had no love for Jews. I could not see him urinating on a Jew if one burst into flames in front of him. Why did he try to save this one?

Pontius Pilate regarded me briefly and with some irritation, like he would a pesky insect.

"Just who is being investigated here, Tribune?" he asked suspiciously. "The Galilean or myself? If you are attempting to uncover some unlawful act on my part for a report to Rome, be aware that there are worse places than Judea where you might find yourself stationed. Places so remote that they have never heard of your family name, nor care whose son you are."

I thought it best not to respond to this, but waited for his ire to right itself. It did.

Pilate's features softened slightly and I knew what was next.

"Of course the reverse is also true," he remarked, beginning to purr like a cat. "If you can bring this problem to a successful conclusion, it would reflect very favourably on you in my report to Rome." He let the last word hang in the air. "I could practically guarantee your request for a change of assignment to anywhere in the Empire. Yes, I dare say, you may even be granted an assignment in *caput mundi*."

And there it was, the threat and the bribe—the very heart of Roman diplomacy.

"As to your last question of 'why?'," Pilate continued, "I have no interest in seeing an innocent man, be he Roman, Jew or other, put to death needlessly. Especially this man in particular."

I was not certain what he meant by this last part, but decided not to pursue it.

"To appease the Jewish leaders I ordered the man flogged, but that was not good enough for them—they wanted him dead. I decided to try another way around it. I told the Hebrew populace that during their Passover holiday it is traditional that as Governor I may release a Jewish prisoner. I gave the people a choice: I could release Jesus or the rebel Barabas. They chose Barabas.

"As a politician I have to recognize expediency. I fell back on an old Roman axiom, 'give the people what they want'."

"So it was a decision made *ad captandum vulgus*," I commented with a hint of contempt. "In order to win over the masses."

"They were calling me a traitor to Caesar!" Pilate stated, and there was a hint of fear under his anger now. "Me, a traitor to Caesar! I did not need any grief over this. Better to be done with it. I handed Jesus over to be crucified and washed my hands of the entire affair." In an unconscious gesture he studied his hands.

"After the crucifixion you called the centurion, Lucius Drusus," I stated in an attempt to draw the Prefect back into the conversation. "You questioned the centurion if Jesus were dead. Why was that?"

Pontius Pilate lowered his hands into his lap, and looked away. He winced as if trying to recall the incident I mentioned. "Ah, yes," he said. "There was a request made by a Hebrew from Arimathea. This man wished to have the body of Jesus for burial. Before allowing him to take the body I thought it prudent to make certain Jesus was dead."

"And you allowed the Arimathean to take the body?"

"Yes."

"Why?" I asked. Pilate regarded at me with hostility and I attempted to explain my reasoning to avoid any misunderstanding. "Did you know this man? Did he claim kinship with Jesus? What was his interest in the body?"

Pilate turned to me with contempt. "It was a simple request, Tribune. I did not see any reason to refuse."

"Yes, but—"

Pilate stared at me steadily for the first time. "We are finished here, Tribune."

I paused briefly, turned on my heels and left the room.

As I walked down the corridor, I reconsidered Pilate's story and how inconsistent it all seemed. I knew for a fact that he did not like the high priests, and that he could have gone against their wishes just to spite them. Yet, if he genuinely wished to spare the Nazarene's life, why send him to the tetrarch Herod, and what was it Herod had said to Jesus?

I was mulling all this over and considering my next move when my attention was caught by a servant girl. She was young and eager-looking. There was urgency in her manner that seemed underlined by fear.

"My mistress wishes to speak to you," she said in a hushed tone. Her eyes darted back and forth along the hallway as if afraid to be seen with me.

"And who is your mistress?" I asked.

"The great lady of the house," she replied. "It is important that she see you."

I turned to leave, but the girl grabbed me by the arm with more strength than I gave her credit for having.

"I will be whipped if I do not bring you to her," the girl spoke in a way that told me she had no intention of letting me leave.

I looked at her. She was beautiful for her age, and would soon become a fine woman that most men would appreciate.

"I would be displeased to see anyone as young and beautiful as you beaten," I told her smiling, but the compliment had little effect.

She led me to an interior room that was ill lit. I turned to say something to her, but she was already gone. Her small bare feet had made no noise upon the floor. The room appeared to be empty, but after a moment I sensed another's presence. A small brazier burned near me. It made more smoke than light. It burned heavy incense, and its low flame threw flickering shadows. I moved past the brazier and let my eyes adjust to the dim light. A figure moved in the far corner of the room. A woman stepped forward out of the shadows. She stood tall and slender, and her black hair was piled high atop her head which made her appear taller than she was. By all the gods, she was beautiful. She reminded me of a statue of Venus I had once seen as a boy in Rome. I had believed it was the most beautiful thing I had ever seen, and for years to come I would use it as a standard from which to compare all other women. Of all the women I had met in my life, no woman could compare to the perfection of Venus. The one who stood before me now came close.

"You know who I am?" she uttered, her voice low and soft.

I nodded. She was Claudia Procula, wife of the Governor, Pontius Pilate.

"You spoke with my husband?"

I nodded.

"Regarding the Galilean, Jesus?"

I nodded.

"What did my husband tell you?"

"Your husband said he did not wish to persecute the Galilean," I told her. "But the man wound up just as dead."

She thought on this a moment. Her lovely face was pensive, and as she spoke she seemed distracted. "Do you know why my husband wished to free Jesus?"

"Your husband told me he could find no guilt in the man."

"That may well be so," she remarked nodding. "I personally do not believe Jesus was guilty of any crime. It was I who asked my husband not to persecute the man."

"Why did you do that?" I asked curiously. "You admitted that you did not know the man."

She turned away from me and paced the room contemplatively. She was dressed in a splendid gown of white and red that swept the dark tile floor. It hung on her well, displaying a fine figure. She turned and faced me again.

"It was a dream," she said.

"It was a what?"

"I had a dream regarding the man Jesus."

"What sort of dream was it?"

"A very disconcerting dream."

"What happened in the dream?" I asked hoping she could be more specific.

"I do not know," she responded confused and bewildered and a little afraid. For some reason I believed what she said; as strange as it sounded. "Or perhaps more to the point, I do not remember. Of the dream I cannot recall precise details. It all becomes cloudier as days pass. All that I can remember is that the dream was disturbing, and it convinced me of the man's innocence. No, more than innocence, he was…he is…"

She did not finish, as if she were uncertain. She gripped my right arm firmly to impress her sincerity. I felt her fingernails sink into my flesh. Her lovely green eyes looked deep into my eyes. By all the gods, she was beautiful! The fierce desperation and concern made her more desirable to me. But she was the Governor's wife, and even I had my limits. They were spelled out in an ancient code of conduct passed down through the ages. Mostly I thought they were a pain in the *podex*.

"Promise me you will be careful," she pleaded. "I fear you are in peril." Here she lifted her hand to the cuts and bruises on my face. She ran her fingers over them gently, caressing them, as if that would heal them. "Promise me!" she repeated.

Apparently she possessed oracle powers, but seemed very ill-at-ease with them, as if not at all certain what to do with them.

"I promise," I responded, then asked her: "What can you tell me of the Jewish tetrarch, Herod?"

"Herod." She said the name like it had been on her mind.

"Your husband, the Governor, sent the man Jesus to Herod, but the tetrarch sent Jesus back to the Governor."

"A strange man," she commented, and for a moment I was not certain to whom she referred. "I cannot tell you much about Herod," she said, and her face held a haunted look. "But one thing did strike me."

"What was that?"

"It has to do with his relationship with my husband"

"Between Herod and the Governor?" I asked, wishing to be specific.

"Yes. They used to be political enemies. They did not even like each other personally. But since the crucifixion of Jesus, they have grown closer, friends even."

"What may have brought them together?" I wondered aloud.

Claudia Procula did not reply but only looked at me. After a moment she said: "Tribune, I understand that in Rome you are *persona non grata*. May I ask you why?"

"It is an extremely personal matter," I said, and would say no more about it.

She nodded. "You may not be welcomed in Rome, Tribune, but please know that you are always welcome here in this house—any time."

Without another word, I left the woman—no easy feat since she evidently desired my company. This last bit of information regarding Herod and Pilate was intriguing. It spoke of conspiracy. The entire matter did. So many players and so many stories. It reminded me of the building of a fantastic mosaic I witnessed once as a child in Rome. The construction of the mosaic began in the centre and grew outward. Each day more tiles were laid, some white, some coloured. At the beginning I saw nothing, simply tiles laid together, side by side. Then I saw a shape, but not a recognizable shape. Then one day, near completion, I saw it. A picture was in the tiles and had become clear to my eyes. I thought it was wondrous. All that time I had seen no discernible pattern or shape, but suddenly it became something. It was a beautiful thing to witness. At this point in time the mystery of the empty tomb was like that mosaic—pieces, hundreds of pieces with no discernible shape. But if I put together enough tiles I would have a clear picture.

CHAPTER IX

▼

To have a clear picture of this mosaic, I first required an audience with the tetrarch, Herod Antipas. Herod's palace was on the western wall. From my quarters in the north part of Jerusalem I made my way through the markets to get to Zion in the Upper City. As I neared the viaduct, I turned down a quiet, narrow street. From somewhere far off I heard the sound of someone calling my name. It was a hushed and unidentifiable voice. I looked up and down the street but saw no one. After my attack the previous night, I felt a bit uneasy. It was midday and I did not imagine anyone would attempt to assault me in the middle of the city in broad daylight. Still, I intended to be wary. I placed my hand inside my tunic and let it rest on the handle of my dagger. I approached a darkened doorway. As I stepped closer, I drew my dagger from its sheath. The familiar bone handle felt reassuring. I lunged forward and grabbed the man who stood in the shadow, and brought the knife to his throat.

"Maximus! Don't kill me!"

"Jupiter! Blind Man!" I exclaimed. "What are you doing here?"

"Trying not to get killed," he whimpered. I could feel him trembling in my grasp.

"You know what I mean," I said, putting my dagger back in its sheath, but still holding onto him with one hand. "Why were you calling me like that?"

"I didn't want anyone to hear. I don't want anyone to see us together."

"You fool, I could have…." I did not know what to say. My nerves were still shaky, but I did not want him to know it.

"What happened to your face?" he asked regarding me closely.

"I walked into a column."

"How many times?"

"What are you doing here?" I asked, perturbed, and finally released him.

"I needed to talk to you."

"About what?"

"I'm having difficulty finding the followers of Jesus."

"And that's what was so urgent you had to find me and tell me?"

"I did learn something."

"What?"

"In regards to one of the disciples, Judas Iscariot."

I had learned that Judas Iscariot was the one who betrayed Jesus, and of all the disciples, he was the one I wished to speak with the most.

"What about him? Do you know where I can find him? Can I speak with him?"

"No."

"Why not?"

"Judas Iscariot is dead."

"What? Dead? How?"

"He either hung himself or he died in a fall. It all depends who you talk to."

"What do you believe?"

"I believe he's dead."

"Any indication he was murdered?"

"Not that I can find."

"Did you discover anything else?"

"Yes. I think I'm getting close to finding that woman Mary you're look for."

"Let me know when you do," I told him. "And Blind Man."

"Yes?"

"Don't ever do that again."

I tossed him a coin and considered giving him a clout on the head for wasting my time, but then thought better of it.

It was always disappointing to discover one of the major conspirators was dead. I was not certain what role Judas Iscariot played, but I suspected it was more than simply a traitor to Jesus. The man knew something. Perhaps he could not live with what he knew and killed himself, or he was killed so he could not reveal what he knew and made to appear as if he took his own life. Either way, Judas Iscariot was like a blind alley—no way out—and I would have to search for answers elsewhere.

Herod's palace in Jerusalem was a grand structure. He always did things in a big way.

His father had been Herod the Great, the infamous Hebrew king, who had wanted a family dynasty and so created his own. Herod the Great had ten wives and at least as many sons. Three of the sons were executed, one disinherited, one banished. It was a scheming, incestuous family who thought nothing of killing one another for love, power, or simply self-preservation. The old patriarch was a cagey, political animal who could juggle allies and enemies, treaties and alliances. He wove a complicated web of intrigue with himself at its centre like a giant spider. But the old man's blood was poisoned with paranoia, and he died an agonizing, ugly death. He was a vindictive sort, for before he died he commanded well-renown Jews from his kingdom to come to him. They were shut up in the hippodrome with orders that upon his death all of them were to be executed so that no one would be happy on the day of his passing, and thus guarantee the country to be in deepest mourning. As brutal as that seemed, Herod the Great outdid himself. With his dying breath, before raving madness overcame him, he ordered his bodyguards to kill his own son Antipater. This last action prompted Augustus Caesar to comment, 'It is better to be Herod's pig than his son.'

I was not certain Herod Antipas would even see me. I waited in an outer room for a good part of the day before being granted an audience.

Like the palace, the audience hall was large and ornate, supported by tall, fat columns with intricate carvings. The painted walls resembled marble, and the floor was of polished imported marble with a decorative mosaic in the centre. Bright coloured curtains hung from the walls decoratively, while at the same time concealed passageways.

Herod sat upon his throne on a raised dias. His regal robes were red and white and tied with gold clasps near his left shoulder. His appearance was more Roman or Greek than Hebrew. I had heard that his grandfather was not even Hebrew, but had converted out of convenience. Next to him on an identical throne sat his wife, Herodias, who had been married to one of Herod Antipas's disinherited stepbrothers. Herodias herself was the daughter of another of her present husband's stepbrothers. This was one close family. Herodias wore her raven tresses pinned up but allowed some strands to hang down on one side; a style that was popular with younger women. She was a full-bodied, mature woman who, as it appeared to me, was desperately trying to hold on to the beauty of her youth. She was still an attractive woman, but her attempts at recapturing her youthful beauty only made her appearance grotesque. Too much makeup and too much jewellery did more harm than good to enhance her looks. But there was no disguising her ambition. The woman coveted power, and meant to hold on to it.

"Ah, Tribune Maximus, you grace us with your presence," Herod Antipas greeted me nobly. It was not all pretence. The man respected everything Roman, and realized no sign of respect to the Empire went unnoticed. "What do we owe the honour of this all too rare visit?" He was all smiles and good cheer, which gave me cause to be wary. Even as he spoke the smile remained on his lips as if he were not speaking with his mouth, the words somehow escaping through his teeth.

"Noble Herod, I am looking into the missing body of one of your people who was crucified Friday last," I told him, but even as I did, I felt the tetrarch knew exactly why I was here. "Before his sentence the man was brought before you."

Herod stopped smiling long enough to don a thoughtful look. He stroked his beard as if that aided his memory. As he recalled the instance, he smiled again and said: "Yes, I remember him. A Galilean of no importance, though he was what you Romans would call *aura popularis*—the popular breeze. But as you know, Tribune, breezes subside. He was reputed to be a great healer and miracle worker, but the man turned out to be a colossal disappointment."

"In what way?" I asked.

Herod cast a sidelong glance at his wife and responded: "We hoped the man would provide us with some amusement, some entertainment. We were in hopes that the man would perform one or two of his miracles for us. I had never seen a miracle, and I was so looking forward to it."

"And did he?"

"Did he what?"

"Did he perform a miracle for you?" I asked.

"No," Herod replied flatly, the smile falling from his lips. "The man refused to perform any acts. He would not even speak. We took it as a personal insult and sent him on his way."

I was about to speak when I heard the sound of movement from behind a rather large column to my left. I looked to the column and saw nothing. I looked to Herod who looked back as if he heard nothing, but I suspected he had.

"You sent Jesus back to Pontius Pilate," I said, more of a statement than question.

"Yes. And it was the Governor who condemned the man in the end. Roman justice, Tribune. The man's death is not on my hands."

"But it was Pilate who sent Jesus to you in the first place," I remarked not entirely certain where I was going with this.

"Yes."

"How is your relationship with the Governor?"

The look on the tetrarch's face betrayed him. He wondered what I knew, and how much I knew.

"The Governor and I are politically amicable. We have not always seen things the same, but we manage to get along with each other."

"Is there anything you can tell me regarding Jesus, or the circumstances of his arrest?"

At this question Herod's jaw went slack and he regarded me with a blank stare. He had, it appeared, inherited some of his father's craft and cunning. He was calculating, in that political mind of his, just how much he should tell me of what he knew. I had come to learn that most people never told me the entire truth. They always held something back for one reason or another. Perhaps they were afraid of incriminating themselves in some way, or that they may accidentally tell someone else's secret. Not that they always cared about getting someone else into trouble, especially if it took attention away from them.

"What time was Jesus brought here?" I asked.

Herod stroked his beard again. "It was late. I do not recall the exact hour. It was late."

"Did you not think that was peculiar?" I asked. "That a man would be brought to you so late?"

"No," he answered proudly. "The affairs of state cannot always wait for daylight. When I am called, I answer the call."

"*Amicus humani generis*," I noted with some sarcasm.

Herod smiled, not noting the sarcasm and said: "Let us say a public servant."

"But you were awake when Jesus was brought," I commented.

"Yes. I often keep late hours."

"And he was brought here under guard."

"Yes."

"You intimated others were present during the man's questioning."

"Yes."

"Who?"

At this question Herod involuntarily glanced at the column to his right, then back to me. This time I was certain I heard something, and so did he. It may have been a soft gasp, and the light step of a sandalled foot upon the floor. I moved stealthily to the column and stepped around to the back of it. No one was there. But there was a trace of scent in the air—nard, imported from India—very expensive.

"Annas and Caiaphas, the high priests were here," Herod blurted out trying to regain my attention—or to draw me away from the column. He knew who had stood behind that column, of that I was certain. I was just as certain he would not say.

I asked Herod: "Is there nothing else you can tell me of the man Jesus?" Herod shook his head, then I said: "Some say the man Jesus was calling himself King of the Jews. Others were beginning to refer to him as such. Did you feel that threatened your position in any way? After all, you are the tetrarch—which is similar to a king—and along came this man who was usurping your title. That must have troubled you greatly."

Herod motioned to answer, but it was his wife, Herodias, who spoke up with no little resentment.

"Tribune, you are obviously referring to the *titulus* the Governor ordered placed on the dead man's cross. We did petition the Prefect regarding this. We told him that the Nazarene only claimed to be the King of the Jews, not that he was in truth the king. For reasons of his own, and known only to himself, Pontius Pilate refused to change the *titulus*."

"Yes, but..." I began to respond, and Herodius raised her hand in objection.

"Tribune, my husband has already told you everything he knows," she spoke haughtily. "This entire affair is insignificant and concerns us not at all. Your questions hint at improprieties on my husband's part, in which case we take grievous offence."

"My apologies, madam," I spoke, trying not to be too humble.

I bowed slightly and turned to leave, then reconsidered and turned back to the tetrarch "If I may ask one last question?" Herod nodded his assent. "How is it you find yourself in Jerusalem at this time?"

"We are here for Passover," he remarked. "It is an important time for us, but we shall soon be leaving for Galilee." Herod cocked his head and regarded my physical appearance. "Now, may I ask you a question, Tribune? What happened to you? You look as if you met up with someone who did not agree with you."

"Yes," I said. "Perhaps they did not like it that I ask so many questions."

"It is never good to ask too many questions, Tribune. A man's personal business is no one's affair but his own."

"Whatever takes place in Jerusalem *is* my concern," I stated.

"Then you may find that a very dangerous affair, indeed," remarked Herod ominously. "Good day, Tribune."

CHAPTER X

▼

I left Herod's palace and wandered through the district of tradesmen; down the streets of butchers, bakers, and ironsmiths, then past the wool-makers, the carders and spinners. I searched halfheartedly for Blind Man because I did not believe he could have made much progress in finding the followers of Jesus in such a short time. It had been a long day, and in some way I felt no closer to the solution than when I started.

By the time I reached my quarters it was getting dark. I was thinking of a cup of wine and my bed. I did not know if Ruth would be there or not. Perhaps it would be best if she were not. I would not be good company tonight. I never was when in the middle of one of these assignments, especially when things were going badly. I entered my quarters. The room was dark except for a lamp that burned low. I stopped in the middle of the room. Someone was there. I could feel their presence more than I could see it or hear it. I sniffed the air. There was a trace of scent—nard, imported from India—very expensive. I knew it did not belong to Ruth. I looked around the room. A piece of woman's clothing lay on the floor. I knew it did not belong to Ruth. Picking it up I held it to my nose and found it carried the nard scent. A silhouette moved on the couch across the room. I walked over to the lamp and used it to light another that brightened the room considerably. Stretched out on my couch was a girl. It was difficult to guess her age. She seemed somewhere between young woman and child, but her entire demeanour exuded sensuality. She lay stretched out on her side, her small sandalled feet and thin ankles crossed. Her upper torso was raised, propped upon one elbow, while the other arm she held akimbo. Her hair was black as night, her bangs cut straight across in the current Egyptian fashion. She was heavily made up and over adorned with jewellery. She was made up to look older than she was. I remembered seeing an older version of her earlier trying to appear younger than she was. She looked at me languidly through half-closed lids, and her red lips were pursed.

"Which of us is in the wrong room?" I said attempting to sound witty and urbane, but once I heard the words spoken aloud, I realized how feeble they sounded.

"I thought you would never get here," she said. Her voice was inviting, like a scorpion enticing its prey.

"I went for a walk after I left Herod's palace," I told her, and saw that it surprised her.

"I did not know you saw me at the palace."

"Hiding behind the column," I finished for her. "Do you enjoy eavesdropping on other people's conversations?"

She did not answer but turned away with a pouting look. I cast the piece of clothing I still held in her general direction. I walked over to a small table and poured myself a cup of wine. As I raised the cup to my lips she said: "You might offer me some wine."

I put down my cup and poured another. Turning I held it out to her. She stretched out her hand with no intention of coming to get it. I carried both cups across the room, and offered one to her. She took it and raised it to her mouth for a taste.

"Very bad wine," she commented.

"Thank you," I said and sat next to her on the couch. She did not move over but brushed up against me. "How did you get in here?" I asked her.

"I had no trouble," she replied proudly and matter of fact. "I simply asked where Tribune Maximus lived and they told me."

"Who told you?"

"Some men. Men just naturally want to help me."

"Of that I am certain."

"I did not know you saw me at the palace," she said smiling coyly.

"I did not see you at the palace," I told her, bringing her down a notch. "Were you hiding behind a column the night the man Jesus was brought before your father?"

"He is not my father," she remarked with some annoyance. "He is my mother's husband. And yes, I was there when Jesus was brought before Herod."

"What was he like?"

"He was a bore," she commented, pouting, then smiled and said: "Not like you. I find you very exciting."

"Oh yes, I am simply fascinating. Now, tell me of the night Jesus was brought before Herod."

"Why must we speak of this?" she said running her fingers up and down my bare arm.

I cocked my head and regarded her closely. "What is your name?" I asked.

"Salome."

"Salome, I need to know these things. Now, on the night Jesus was brought before Herod, who was present?"

Salome thought a moment and spoke: "Besides Herod, my mother and I were there, as was Annas, Caiaphas, some members of the court, and half a score of guards."

"Roman guards or Temple guards?"

"Both."

"Continue."

"The man was brought in under guard. He was questioned. He was asked to perform some magic."

"And did he?"

"No. He did not cooperate in any way. He would not speak. He would not do anything asked of him."

"Did he appear anxious or nervous at all?"

"No. He appeared as if he did not care about anything. He did not even seem to care when Herod's guards mocked him."

"What did they do to him?"

"One guard struck him on the face with an open hand. Everyone thought it was amusing when they put a royal robe on him. He reminded me of…"

She let the words drift off without completing her thought.

"He reminded you of who?" I prompted her.

Salome seemed reluctant to speak. She would not even meet my eyes.

I held her chin between thumb and forefinger and turned her head to meet my gaze. "He reminded you of who?" I repeated gently.

"He reminded me of another man who was brought before Herod some time ago," she continued, but her voice was subdued and strangely soft. "The other man's name was John. Some called him John the Baptist. He said some mean things about my mother, and Herod had the man arrested and put to death. Herod must have felt guilty about executing John, for he thought this Jesus was the spirit of John come back to vex him. Have you ever heard of anything so ridiculous?"

She tried to make light of it, but I could tell by her manner she was disturbed by the affair.

"Who was this John?" I asked her.

"A desert madman. A self-proclaimed profit," Salome said with disdain. "He spoke wild utterances, and I heard he tried to drown people in the Jordan. He even looked like a madman. He was dressed in camel hair and smelled bad."

"What was it about this man, John, that disturbed you?"

"I told you; he spoke against my mother!"

"Did he say anything that was untrue?"

Anger flashed in those beautiful green eyes. This one could be a wildcat, I thought to myself.

"Whatever he may have said against my mother reflected upon me," she said with some vehemence. "Who was he to judge her or me? He deserved to die!"

As quickly as her ire had risen, it dissipated to be replaced by a soothing charm that would do justice to a cobra. She gazed at me through those half-closed lids and ran the fingers of her right hand along the rim of my left ear.

"Let us talk of something else, darling," she whispered, and her voice was enticing. "You know, you are quite handsome, in a rough sort of way. I like the scars on your face. Did your woman give you those? Do you like it rough? I like it rough."

The spectacle she put on disgusted me, and I was not giving her the response she expected. "Do you not find me desirable, my handsome Roman tribune?" she asked, her tone changing slightly. "Do I need to dance for you? Is that what I need to do to get you interested? Do not tell me a big Roman soldier like you has trouble with his sword. Is that it? Is it a big sword, or just a little dagger?"

Salome reached between my legs. I grabbed her tightly by the wrist and brought the wrist up twisting it slightly. She grimaced in pain, and that fiery hate leapt back into her eyes. As Salome struggled to break free, she brought up her other hand to strike me with it. I caught at that wrist also and held them both in my right hand. Her head shot forward and she sank her teeth into the knuckles of my hand. She made low animal noises as she bit down hard. I clenched my teeth to keep from crying out in pain, then I shoved her away from me as hard as I could. Salome landed on the floor in a sprawl. As quick as a cat she was on all fours glaring up at me with her hair entangled hanging in her face, her lips pulled back, revealing a bestial snarl, and that look of utter hatred in her wild eyes. All civilized manner was gone from her entire being, and I was quite certain she wanted to kill me—would have killed me if given half a chance. I looked at the back of my right hand. The teeth-marks were clearly visible and deep. A small trickle of blood was running from the wound. I looked at Salome with disgust.

"Little girl, you leave here now under your own power, or with the help of my foot."

She remained on the floor for a brief moment judging my character, and if I were capable. Slowly she stood up, collected whatever loose clothing lay about and departed.

I got out Ruth's oils and began to clean the wound from the bite. A short time later Ruth arrived. In my mind I imagined what might have occurred had she come home a bit earlier. Silently I thanked the gods for my good fortune. Ruth came to me and took over the cleaning of my wound.

"What happened?" she asked concerned.

"I got bit," I told her simply, and felt certain she would not press the issue.

"This is a human bite mark," she observed. Ruth sniffed the air, then leaned closer to me and sniffed again. "Who was she?"

I did not answer, certain she would not press the issue.

"Who was she?" Ruth repeated.

I gave her my 'she who?' look. As soon as I did, I knew it was a mistake.

Ruth took my right hand and threw it down into my lap. She stood up and stormed off.

"She was neither invited nor welcomed," I called after Ruth, hoping that would appease her.

Ruth picked up something and threw it at me in disgust. I decided to give her that one, so I allowed the object to hit me in the face. It was a strong throw and the object stung a bit when it struck me. It dropped to the floor, and I stooped to pick it up. Holding it in my hand, I examined the object. It was a long, studded leather strap with a bit of metal dangling for one end. I knew I had seen some like it before.

"Where did this come from?" I asked Ruth, who looked as if she were leaving. I ran over to her and grabbed her. Spinning her around I held the object in front of her face. "Where did you get this?" I asked again with enough force to let her know it was important.

Ruth looked at me with a mixture of concern and curiosity. She looked at the leather strap, then back to me. "From you," she spoke with angry frustration. "I got it from you. What is it and why is it important?"

"What do you mean you got it from me? When?"

Ruth shook her head confused, trying to think straight through a maze of emotions.

"You brought it home with you," she said. "You had it clutched in your hand. I had to force your hand open for you to release it."

"When?" I asked. "When did I come home with this clutched in my hand?"

"You had it with you that night. The night when you came home drunk and beaten."

It took me a brief moment to figure it out. It took me a few more moments to formulate a plan. It took me much longer to convince Ruth to help me with my plan. She was still upset with me, but I needed her. It did not occur to me to tell her so.

CHAPTER XI

▼

There are several establishments in and around Jerusalem where men may go after a long and tiring day to relax and find comfort in the arms of a woman—or any number of women. The Roman soldiers of Antonia Fortress frequented a certain place, and any given number could be found there on any given night. Soldiers tended to stick together, even when they went out to satiate their sexual appetites. Septimus Flavius was at such a place with his companions Marius, Titus and Scarus.

According to the centurion, Lucius Drusus, Septimus Flavius was a good soldier. One benefit in joining the Roman legion was an opportunity to see the world. Unlike some of his fellow legionaries, Flavius did not mind Judea. He found the climate tolerable and the people hospitable: or was it the other way around? He was not from the best family in Rome. His family was not nearly the richest nor the most influential. He had not joined the Roman legion to uphold his family name or to make a name for himself. He knew he was not the hero type, and would not find fame or great fortune here. He would undoubtedly live out his days in obscurity, perhaps rising a modicum in rank. His companions were not the best nor were they the worst, so he would stick with them—for now. Although, once he felt they were leading him to ruin, he would cut all ties with them. For the time being they all shared a secret that bound them together, but for how long Flavius did not know.

Septimus Flavius took a drink of the cheap wine offered in the bawdyhouse. So far, all three of his companions had lain with women this night. Scarus had done so twice and would soon be working on his third. Flavius was a trifle more particular, a bit more shy, and certainly less driven. He liked older women. They reminded him of his mother. As a younger man he had often imagined himself lying with her.

The woman he looked at now was not older, nor did she remind him of his mother, but she had been staring at him all evening. If nothing else Flavius did find Hebrew women most appealing—they were mysterious and exotic. The one who exchanged looks with him now was a dark-haired, dark-eyed beauty who did not appear to need much encouragement. Flavius took a drink of wine for courage before he approached her. He was not inexperienced, but he felt nervous every time. With his companions close by Flavius felt he had to display all the bravado he could muster. As he approached the woman, he looked her up and down and drank in every detail. She was shapely, young and beautiful, and she eyed him seductively. They stood close and he let his hand rest on her shoulder. She smiled and leaned in closer to let her long eyelashes brush his cheek. He felt her breath on his face. Flavius was ensnared, and it was now only a matter of time. She whispered in his ear, and he felt the nape of his neck bristle. She suggested that they leave and find a more private place, a place where they could take their time. He found he could not speak but only nod his head. She took him by the hand and led him away from his friends, like a lamb being led to slaughter. Flavius never suspected a thing. She led him to a quiet, out of the way spot, out of earshot, away from everything. It was a small, humble dwelling, sparsely furnished. The dwelling was typical of Judea—a cube-shaped building of whitewashed, oven-dried brick, with a dirt floor, and flat roof of hard packed clay. Flavius never truly noticed this, he was concentrating on the woman. He never knew what hit him. It was a small rock to the back of the head. Flavius stiffened and hit the ground like a statue being pushed over.

Ruth gasped and I dropped the rock to the ground. She took a step back and stared at the prone Flavius.

"Did you kill him?" Ruth asked in a frightened whisper.

"It was just a tap," I said, and paused to look at her. She was dressed in her old working clothes. I had not seen her made up like this for some little time. It brought back memories of when we first met, and why I was attracted to her in the first place.

"This must remind you of old times," I remarked smiling, but she did not smile back.

"I do not wish to recall those days," she shot back at me with a vicious look. "I vowed to never return to that life."

"But you were so good at it," I commented sincerely, hoping it would make her feel good about herself. It did not.

"I promised to help you, and I did," Ruth said rather stiffly. "I am leaving now."

I watched her walk away. I went to say something, but figured it would not come out right, so I let her go. I turned back to Flavius, who lay moaning on the ground. I grabbed him by his tunic and propped him up with his back resting against the wall of the dwelling. Snatching up a short wooden stool, I placed it next to him on his left. I sat upon it facing the man with my left foot upon his right wrist and my right foot resting upon his chest. Taking out the long, studded leather strap, I began to slap Flavius in the face with it, lightly at first, then a little harder with each slap until he began to regain consciousness. Flavius moved his face from side to side in attempts to avoid the blows. As he came awake, he instinctively brought up his free hand to protect his face from the strap. He swore an oath and his eyes opened wide to look at me with a mixture of anger and surprise.

"Tribune!" he half shouted. "What are you doing!?"

"Attempting to rouse you," I said.

"You succeeded!" he stated, then brought up his free hand to the back of his head. He touched it and winced with pain. "What happened?"

"I hit you on the head with a rock."

His eyes narrowed and his face contorted with bewilderment. "Why!?" he demanded, and for the first time realized I had a foot on his wrist and chest. "What is going on!?" he wanted to know.

"I needed to get you alone away from your friends so we could talk in private," I told him.

"What about?" he said. Not all the bravado had been knocked out of him. He still believed he had some control. I needed him to know he had none. I hit him across the face with the leather strap. He started.

"I am going to ask you some honest questions and you are going give me some honest answers," I informed him.

"Let me go!" Flavius said, and motioned to get up.

I leaned forward and put my weight on his wrist and chest. Then I slapped him again.

"It was you and your companions who attacked me the other night, wasn't it?" I remarked.

He did not answer, so I struck him again.

"It was you and the others."

"No!"

SLAP!

"Why do you believe it was us?" he wanted to know.

"I came home with this clutched in my hand," I said to him, holding the leather strap before his eyes. "Do you know what it is?" No answer.

SLAP!

"Yes, I know what it is," he admitted.

"It is from the apron worn by a Roman soldier," I stated. "The round marks on my body I received from the beating are from the hobnails on the bottom of sandals worn by Roman soldiers. The four of you tried to stomp me into the ground."

"It was not us," he said subdued.

SLAP!

"You four were the only soldiers I questioned that day," I stated.

"It was not us."

SLAP!

"All right! It was us," Flavius admitted.

"Why did you attack me?"

No answer.

SLAP!

"All right! I will tell me if you stop striking me!" he said. I eased up on him. Flavius took a breath and looked away. "You worried us when you came around asking questions about the Nazarene."

"Why?"

No answer. You think he would have learned by now.

SLAP!

"We were told to keep our mouths shut," he admitted.

"Told by whom?"

"Caiaphas."

"The high priest?"

"Yes."

"What did he want you to keep your mouths shut about?"

"He did not want us to speak about what happened at the Nazarene's tomb."

"You all lied to me before, didn't you," I said. "The followers of Jesus did not come and steal his body, did they."

Flavius shook his head—not so much as a denial, but almost as if he were not entirely certain what had taken place.

"I want you to tell me exactly what happened at that tomb," I told him slowly and deliberately.

Flavius took a long pause before he began.

"We were given orders to guard the tomb. It seemed ridiculous to us—guard a dead man's tomb. We were told the orders came down from Pontius Pilate, but we knew Caiaphas was behind it, the same way we knew that when we were ordered to arrest Jesus in the garden, they were, in truth, the wishes of the high priest. After the crucifixion Caiaphas and his kind were afraid that Jesus's followers would come and steal away the body, and claim he had risen from the dead in hopes people would believe him to be the Hebrew messiah. Later, after the…incident, we were told that if questioned, we were to say that that was exactly what happened."

"But that was not what happened," I remarked.

Flavius shook his head. "No," he said, and his entire demeanour now changed. He became quiet, and a little afraid.

"Tell me everything from the beginning," I said.

Flavius looked at me. His face was sombre and his eyes watery. When he spoke, his voice was calm and low, but held a hint of regret in its coarseness.

"We were with the group that went to the garden in Gethsemane the evening of *dies Jovis*—Thursday, to arrest Jesus—Marius, Titus, Scarus and myself. By the time we reached the garden our numbers had swelled as we were joined by temple guards and priests and slaves. Jesus and his followers were few. Still, as we began to arrest the Nazarene, one of his followers grabbed up a sword and struck at a servant of Caiaphas. The servant was struck upon the ear, and we four prepared for an attack. Just then, Jesus stepped forward and raised a hand to cease the hostilities. He said something about living by the sword and dying by the sword, then he reached out and healed the servant's wound."

"What do you mean 'healed it'?"

"I mean, Tribune, Jesus touched the man's wound and it healed. Later the four of us vowed never to speak of it."

"Why?"

"Because of what happened at the tomb a few days later."

"Tell me what took place at the tomb."

"As we admitted earlier, the four of us were ordered to guard the tomb. That much was true. The part about the high priests suspecting Jesus's followers might steal his body was also true. I believe their fears were genuine."

"Was it also true about drinking on duty?" Flavius nodded and I said: "I need to know exactly what happened."

"It is difficult to explain," Flavius began. "Like Marius said earlier, it was easy duty. We stood guard in shifts; two stayed awake, two slept. We were always there together. For the most part nothing much happened. Some people came around. I recall one older Jew approached the tomb the evening of the crucifixion, but he turned away before he reached it. Our presence might have frightened him off, I do not know. Nothing happened until the morning of *dies solis*—Sunday. It was early, the sun had only begun to rise. I was awake and had been up almost the entire night. I was tired, but could not sleep. Marius was sleeping close by. Titus and Scarus were staring at two women coming towards us. I looked at the women and recognized them from the crucifixion."

"What did they look like?"

"They were Jews. One older, one younger."

"The younger one; did she look like she worked the streets?"

"She was pretty enough," Flavius commented, "but she was not dressed for it. Both were dressed very simply."

"What happened then?"

Flavius swallowed twice and looked at me warily. "The women approached and they were close when it happened."

"When what happened?"

Flavius hesitated again and I motioned for him to continue. "The ground began to shake. It was so violent I could barely keep my feet. Everything was shaking and I saw the stone roll away from the entrance of the tomb."

"Did you see anyone come out of the tomb?" I asked anxiously.

He shook his head and looked at me as if it were a ridiculous question.

"I called to my companions," Flavius said. "Marius was awake by this time, but the shaking seemed to unnerve us all. The three of us who were standing fell to the ground. Once I did, I could not seem to move."

"What do you mean?"

Flavius spoke hesitantly, as if not certain how to describe it. "I felt…overcome…by something…a paralysis that affected my body. I could not move. When I looked at my companions they too seemed similarly afflicted. We simply lay there, unable to move."

"You had been drinking," I reminded him. "Perhaps you suffered from *delirium tremens*, which explained the trembling and the hallucinations."

Flavius shook his head. "We did not drink that much."

Now I had been aware of soldiers being so frightened in battle that they could not move. They could not attack or retreat as the case may be. I asked Flavius if it was like that.

He thought of this for a moment and said: "I do not believe so. Not the way you may think. It was not like that. It was like…"

Flavius could not finish. His face twisted and I truly believe he was going to weep. I gave him a light slap in the face with the leather strap. It seemed to bring him back to himself.

"That one was for your benefit," I said. "Now, you were saying what it was like."

"It was like nothing I have ever experienced, or want to experience again."

"Perhaps the earthquake unnerved you," I suggested.

"No. For even after the ground ceased to shake, we still found ourselves paralysed. We could not move, or speak. But the two women were not affected. They walked right past us."

"What did they do?"

"They approached the tomb, and…and…"

"And what?" I said, and held up the strap. "I do not want to have to use this again."

"You will not believe me," he stated.

"Just say it."

He swallowed hard again and cocked his head as if not certain what to say, or uncertain if he himself believed what he was about to say.

"As the two women walked past us I could not turn to see the tomb, but was aware of a light coming from that direction. The light grew brighter encompassing everything. I thought if I looked at the light it would blind me like the sun. Truth be told, I did not want to look. I was afraid. I was…terrified."

"Of what?"

"I do not know," he answered and began to sob. "Whatever it was, it gripped at my heart."

He ceased talking and I gave him a moment to regain his composure. Flavius did not seem to be any kind of threat to me, so I stood up from my position and he remained on the ground.

"What about the others?" I asked him.

"It was the same for all of us, I am certain. We did not speak of it, even in private. When we could stand, some time later, the women were gone and the tomb was empty. We knew that the high priest wanted the tomb guarded, so we decided to go and see Caiaphas to explain what had occurred. We must have sounded insane. He insinuated that we had been drinking. Marius grew enraged at this and nearly assaulted the man. This must have convinced Caiaphas that we were telling the truth, or at least the truth as we knew it. He looked at us thoughtfully, then left to discuss the matter with the elders. After a time, Caiaphas returned with a group of them and he told us, 'You were right to come

to me regarding this. You are to talk about this with no one. Do you understand?'
We said we did, and Caiaphas emphasized 'no one'. 'Your story will be that the
followers of Jesus came in the night and stole the body from the tomb,' he told
us. We told him we did not like the idea of lying to our commanders, and that we
would be disciplined for failure in our duty. 'If Pilate hears of this, we will per-
suade him of your actions and secure your positions,' Caiaphas told us. To com-
pensate us for our troubles and ensure our cooperation they offered us money. A
great deal of money."

"Did you take it?"

Flavius shrugged and said: "Why not? We figured that if we went around telling anyone the truth, no one would believe us. So we took the Hebrew's money
and later the four of us swore an oath on our lives that none of us would talk
about what happened at the tomb ever again, even amongst ourselves."

"Then I came along asking questions."

"You worried us. Marius said you were trouble. If you were to learn the truth,
it would make our positions very bad. Marius said we had to discourage you from
asking any more questions. He figured if we attacked you pretending to be Jews,
you would give up the chase. We put Hebrew robes on over our uniforms and
followed you. Lucky for us you went out drinking and became easy prey. One
blow from Marius and you went down. We spoke Aramaic to throw you off
guard. We figured you might think Jesus's followers attacked you, and you would
never suspect us. I suppose we were wrong."

"You were wrong all the way through," I said. "You were wrong when you
thought a single beating would cause me to give up. You were wrong when you
thought I would not learn the truth of who attacked me. You were wrong when
you thought I would not learn the truth about what happened at the tomb."

"Then you believe me?"

"Why would you lie now? Besides, I chose you to question in private because
you spoke the least the other day. You were not comfortable with all the lies. You
wanted to tell the truth. If I had brought Marius or either of the other two here, I
would have had to beat them to near death before they would have told me what
really happened.

"One last question," I said. "From where did the goatskin of wine come that
you all drank that night?"

"I believe Marius brought it with him. Why?"

I did not bother to answer.

Flavius did not attempt to hide his shame, then looked at me with trust, and
asked: "Do you believe any of this talk that he was the son of God?" I stared at

Flavius but did not answer. His eyes filled again. "What does it all mean, Tribune?"

"I do not know yet," I said. "But I am going to find out."

CHAPTER XII

▼

Growing up in Rome, I naturally knew all the gods. There was Jupiter, of course, god of rain, thunder and lightning, and sovereign head of the Roman state. Alongside Jupiter was Juno, the protector of women in marriage and childbirth. There was an entire plethora of gods—Apollo, Minerva, Mars, Mercury, Venus, Vulcan, Pluto, and others. Like all good Romans I was raised to pay due respect to the gods, and thus ensure the *pax deorum*—peace of the gods. In every major business venture, in all political moves, in most daily decisions, private citizens honoured the gods in hopes of receiving divine blessings in every aspect of their lives, which would in turn benefit the entire community. In our home, as in every other household in Rome, we had a *lararium*—or altar. At the *lararium* we made small sacrifices of bread, wine, or fruit to the *lares* who were to watch over our family. In my family's case, it would appear, the offerings were not sufficient. Back in Rome, we had countless public festivals to honour the gods, and many temples were built in their names. I grew up respecting the gods, but I was never certain if I truly believed in them. It often occurred to me that if there were gods, they had better things to do than take an interest in our miserable little lives.

After I left Flavius I went back to my quarters. Ruth was not there. I supposed she was still upset with me. I lay in bed and thought on what Flavius told me regarding his experience at the tomb. Any other time I would assume someone was making up such a story. Strangely enough, I believed Flavius was telling the truth…as bizarre as it sounded. The only reasonable explanation for the guards' strange experience was that their wine must have been tampered with so to cause queer and unusual sights. I had, of course, heard of such concoctions before, but I was too tired to think it through tonight so I went to sleep. I had no dreams.

I woke in the morning to find a very unfriendly face staring down at me.

"You look as if you were dragged through Hades," Lucius Servanus spoke. That expression was becoming his typical greeting to me. "What happened—get into a fight?"

"Yes, but you should see the other four," I commented. Truth was, thanks to Ruth's treatment, my cuts were healing and the swelling had gone done considerably.

"Is it me, or is it awfully hot?" I asked wiping beads of sweat from my brow.

"It's you and it's hot," he said. "It is always hot."

Servanus looked about the surroundings with disgust. "So this is where you live," he uttered. If memory served, he had never been to my quarters before, and I could not imagine anything that would bring him here. "I am here to check on your progress regarding the missing corpse—the empty tomb."

"What do you want to know?"

"Have you found the body?" he asked frustrated.

"Not yet."

"How close are you?" I shrugged, and Servanus asked: "Have you found Jesus's disciples?"

"Not yet."

"What in Hades have you been doing?" he demanded angrily.

"My duty," I said simply.

He stabbed a pudgy finger at me and said: "You listen to me, Maximus, you had best get off your ass and bring this affair to a successful conclusion, or you will find yourself buried neck-deep in the dung pile near the south wall of the city. The Governor is anxious to see this matter concluded. Rome wants this matter concluded. Even the Jewish elders want an end to this. Now, what seems to be your problem? Jerusalem is not that big. Why can't you find those disciples?"

"Do you truly want to know, or are you here simply to make my life miserable?" I asked.

"I truly want to know."

"The disciples are in hiding," I told Servanus. "There is no trace of them. Their leader was crucified. They are very likely scared to show their faces. They may have returned to Galilee, or may have fled Jerusalem for parts unknown. They may have joined up with a caravan and be half way to Damascus. They may be on a ship bound for Cyprus. Where do you suggest I start?"

"You have started," the Praetor said sternly. "I hear you have been questioning our own people—the centurion Drusus and four of his men. I do not know what you said to Drusus, but now he is missing."

"What do you mean missing?"

"I mean he is gone. He cannot be found. No word. No trace."

"That is interesting," I said. "But I am too busy to start looking for Drusus also."

"Oh, I know how busy you are," Servanus spat. "I understand you had an audience with the Governor. Why did you feel that you needed to speak with Pilate? And Herod Antipas! What was the point of talking with the tetrarch?"

"Today I am going to see the high priest, Caiaphas."

"Why, for Jupiter's sake?!"

I got out of bed and faced Servanus. "Because they know something—all of them do. They are all hiding something about the man Jesus, and I am going to find out what it is."

"You are the most stubborn man I ever met! Do you know that?"

"Some have said so."

Servanus looked at me strangely. "No, you are not stubborn; you are mad! Do you know that, Maximus? You are a madman! You are going to get yourself in trouble, or worse: dead. You cannot go up against these people, Maximus—they are too powerful. Take a lesson from Publius Ovidius Naso; *bene qui latuit bene vixit.* You pursue this line of investigation and I am going to find your body buried out in the desert somewhere."

"*Alea iacta est,*" I said stubbornly. "The die is cast."

Servanus shook his head in disgust and said: "I cannot talk to you when you get like this. And quoting Julius Caesar will not help you. But I am warning you Maximus; you be careful or one day soon you will end up with your head on a post."

With that cheery comment Servanus departed. I got myself dressed and went out looking for Blind Man to see if he had discovered anything new. Today there were games at the amphitheatre, and Blind Man liked to watch them in secret and bet on the matches.

About fifty-five years ago Herod the Great had the amphitheatre built to hold Roman-style games in honour of his new patron, Caesar Augustus. The amphitheatre was outside Jerusalem, on a large flat level of ground. It was round, like most of the amphitheatres back in Rome, but not as large. Here were held contests of strength, skill, and speed, which allowed athletes to compete in wrestling matches and foot races. These events simply warmed up the spectators for more engaging competition. The feature events of the games generally provided more bloodshed for the crowds. Slaves or condemned criminals were forced to fight to the death, or were pitted against wild beasts. The highlight of the games allowed spectators to view Roman trained gladiators as they pitted their skill against one another. These matches were also to the death, but if a contestant fell wounded he might be spared if the audience decided he fought well. The spectators would signal his fate with a *pollice verso* by turning their thumbs towards their chest to indicate if he should be spared, or with a *pollice compresso* by keeping their thumbs in their fists to signal death to the vanquished. All in all, it was a relaxing way to spend an afternoon.

I searched the amphitheatre for Blind Man, but he was not to be found. I was prepared to leave when I looked over to the preferred seats and spotted Pontius Pilate and Herod Antipas sitting together under the shade of a canopy enjoying the festivities. I recalled Pilate's wife's remark how, in the past, the Governor and the tetrarch had been political enemies, but since the crucifixion they had become almost friends. I observed the two men, and they did appear, in truth, to be enjoying each others company. I wondered what had brought them so close. At one point I observed Herod layed his hand briefly on Pilate's knee, and I wondered if their close relationship was of an unnatural manner.

I decided to have a little fun and obtain some information while I was at it. I grabbed a young boy who was passing by and said to him in an authoritative voice: "Do you know who I am, boy?" The boy, a lad of perhaps ten years of age, shook his head, while his mouth hung open in dumb amazement. "I am Praetor Lucius Servanus. The Governor told me he would be here. He is anxiously await-ing important dispatches from Rome. I must see the Governor in my quarters at once, for the dispatches have just arrived from the Emperor. Find the Governor and tell him it is imperative I see him immediately. Do you understand?"

The boy nodded mutely. I reached into my flat purse and handed him my last coin. The boy accepted it gladly and went off on his way. I took up a position where I could observe the little drama without being seen. A short time later the young boy found Pontius Pilate and explained all I had said. Pilate dawned a con-fused expression as the boy spoke and pointed to where I had been standing. A moment later Pilate addressed Herod in an apologetic manner and left his seat. I waited until Pilate exited the amphitheatre before I walked down the steps to where Herod Antipas sat observing the end of a foot race between five athletes. Herod seemed quite surprised when I took the seat Pilate had just vacated.

"Why, Tribune Maximus!" the tetrarch ejaculated. "What a pleasure it is to see you again so soon."

I smiled knowingly, all the while watching the athletes. The crowd grew louder as the runners sprinted towards the end, and some of the spectators rose to their feet as the contestants crossed the spot that marked the end of the race. I was aware that Herod was more curious of my appearance than he was about the runners.

"A fine race," I remarked as I watched the field and avoided meeting the tetrarch's eyes.

"Do you come to the games often?" Herod asked me.

"Not as often as I'd like," I replied. "Let this be between us, but I do enjoy a small wager on the matches, now and then."

"Do you, really?" Herod said silkily. "Would you care to wager on this next wrestling match?"

Despite the fact that my purse was empty I said: "I would indeed, if only to make our company even more appealing."

Two naked wrestlers enter the arena, one a tall lean man, the other a short but broad shouldered man.

"Just to make this interesting," I added, "I will wager on the little fellow."

Herod laughed and said: "Are you certain?" I nodded and he asked: "And how much do you wish to wager?"

I pursed my lips and winced as if in thought. "How about ten denarii?"

Herod raised his eyebrows. "Are you sure you wish to wager so much?" he queried.

"If you believe it is too much we do not have to wager at all," I said with a wave of my hand.

"No, no. If you wish to, I will cover your wager," Herod said with some satisfaction.

The two wrestlers turned to the audience, saluted, and took their stance to begin the match.

"As long as we are here," I began amicably, "could you tell me about a desert prophet named John the Baptist?"

I observed Herod's features stiffen at hearing the name, and some colour ran out of his face. He licked his lips nervously as his mouth opened and closed, but no words came out. Finally he managed to say: "What do you know of John the Baptist?"

"I know that you had him arrested, locked up and executed. You also thought that Jesus was John the Baptist come back to life."

"How do you know these things?" Herod asked puzzled.

"I am a Roman tribune," I responded taking on a very serious tone. "It is my job to know these things."

"Then you must tell me—" he began, but I cut him off.

"Oh, look," I said. "My man has won."

It was true. Through guile, persistence, and skill, the shorter wrestler had out-maneuvered his taller opponent.

I turned to Herod with an expectant expression. He reached into his purse and counted out ten small silver denarii. Two more wrestlers entered the arena, and I proposed we wager the same amount again to allow him to regain his loss. Grim faced, Herod accepted.

"I will wager upon the man on the left," I announced pointing.

"You chose your man last match," Herod explained. "Please allow me first choice." I nodded and he said: "I will take the man on the left." We shook hands on the wager, and Herod stated: "I would be interested to learn, Tribune, how you know so much about John the Baptist."

"Was I mistaken in anything I said?" I asked innocently. "Did you not have the man executed simply for insulting your wife?"

He looked at me stone-faced, and stressing each word he said: "It was not as simple as that."

"No? That is not what Salome told me."

"Salome!" Herod spat. "Salome, that she-devil! Is that who told you these things?" I nodded and he demanded: "When?"

"Last evening," I said. "She came to my quarters." I added this last part deliberately. It seemed to have the desired effect. The tetrarch's face grew red with rage.

"That scheming little—" he did not finish, but went on to say excitedly. "It was all her doing, you see. I did not want to do it, but she tricked me into it. It was all her fault!"

"Perhaps you had better tell me exactly what happened."

Herod Antipas took in a few deep breaths. His clenched both his hands into tight balls that turned the knuckles white, then released them. He brought up his right hand and stroked his beard.

"You must understand," Herod began speaking low but forceful, "the crown upon my head is heavy."

Now where have I heard that before?

"When you are a king, it is crucial that people know you have power, for if they do not, then you have none. It is always dangerous to show weakness. When the baptizer John came and accused my wife, Herodias, of sinful deeds, I was forced to act. I imprisoned the man. For weeks I kept him locked up, and all the while my wife and her daughter reminded me of how he had insulted them. Well, one evening when I had been drinking too much, I asked Salome to dance for me. Have you ever seen Salome dance, Tribune?" I shook my head. "It is a sight to behold. She moves like gossamer on a breeze. But this night she was obstinate, and refused to dance for me. I was persistent, and she finally agreed if I would give her something in return. I told her I would give her anything, but that was not good enough. She forced me to give my word that I would grant her a wish if she danced. I did not want to give my word. I knew that I should not, but she tricked me somehow, and in front of the entire court I gave my word. Oh, that I could have cut out my tongue before I swore to her. She danced. I do not believe she ever danced more graceful, more seductive than she did that night. And when she finished, Salome came to me, smiling that smile that both excites and frightens me, and she asked to be recompensed for her dance."

"What did she ask?" I queried, intrigued by the man's account.

Herod put his hands to his face and shook his head back and forth. "I cannot tell you."

"Tell me."

"Salome asked for the head of John the Baptist!"

The crowd cheered as the wrestling match ended with a surprising and spectacular move.

"And you granted her request," I said when the noise of the spectators receded.

Herod's eyes were closed as he nodded. "What else could I do?" he moaned. "I am the king and I gave my word."

"Surely men have died by your orders before," I stated. "Why does John the Baptist's death vex you so?"

"I do not know," Herod replied. "The memory of the man haunts me. For some reason the guilt is unbearable."

"It was this guilt that led you to believe the baptizer had come back in the form of Jesus?" I proposed to him. Herod did not answer, and I asked: "Is that why you would take no action against Jesus? Or was it something else?"

I could read guilt and fear in Herod's face, and I suspected I had stumbled upon something close to the truth. Herod looked back at me, and in my face he must have seen that I knew it.

"You may not know this Tribune," he began, "but my father was a great man. He made Jerusalem what it is today. My father built this amphitheatre, the Temple, the hippodrome. If you think the palace here in Jerusalem is impressive, you should behold the three magnificent palaces he built in Jericho. It would be difficult to count all the fortresses and temples my father built. At one time his kingdom stretched from Gaza and Masada to the end of the River Jordan. It is a noble heritage I share. I intend to live up to it. My father worked hard to make this country what it is. I will not dishonour his memory, or what he has bequeathed me. I do not easily give up what is mine."

And there I had my answer.

"It appears that this last match belongs to me," I said smugly, as I held my previous winnings in my hand. With hidden rancour Herod handed over ten more small silver denarii.

"You are quite fortunate, Tribune," he commented with resentment. "You are a good judge of wrestlers."

"Those wrestlers are Roman soldiers," I told him. "I watch them train every day."

Herod's face turned a nice shade of red as he attempted to repress his rage. To fan his rage I said: "As for your father, he was a sick, twisted despot, who died a slow, agonizing death because he had bad blood. Your only heritage is that this same bad blood runs in you."

I stood up and left him with those reassuring words.

CHAPTER XIII

▼

I exited the amphitheatre and continued to search for Blind Man. I found him outside the south wall of the Temple Mount. Both the sun and heat were rising, and I wondered how Blind Man could possibly sit out in them all day long.

"Where have you been?" I asked him.

"Where have I been? Where have *you* been?" he came back at me. "I was searching for you all last evening."

"You found someone?"

"I found Mary."

"Mary Magdalene?!" I said excited.

"Her name is Mary and she knew Jesus. That is all I know."

"Where is she?" I said. Blind Man held out his wooden beggar bowl. I reached into my purse and withdrew one of the silver denarii I had just won.

Blind Man looked at it somewhat surprised, then his gaze shifted to my purse and he wondered how many more denarii were inside.

I looked at him, shaking my head, and said: "You best forget about it. You tell me where I can find this Mary, or when you walk away from here you truly will be blind!"

Needless to say Blind Man gave me the directions of where I could find Mary. It was a fine-looking farmhouse north of the city. It was not exactly like the dwellings in Jerusalem. This one was built of stone and plastered on the outside with clay and lime. The roof was flat made up of reeds and sticks woven together and coated with a thick clay to keep out the rain. No one appeared to be about the place. It was the middle of the day, and I suspected everyone was working in the nearby fields harvesting barley. I pushed on the wooden door of the house. It was not locked, and swung open on creaking leather hinges. It felt cooler inside the house. It was a moderate size dwelling with perhaps several small rooms in its two storeys. I entered the cooking area that consisted of an oven, several pieces of pottery that varied in size, some wooden utensils, and a store of firewood. The room was lit by the strong sunlight that entered through a small, but high window. I walked to the back of the house and out a door that opened onto a sunken courtyard enclosed by a low stone wall. I stood on the back porch that stretched almost the entire length of the house and was shaded by a makeshift roof of sticks and thatch supported by the back wall of the house on one side, and three evenly spaced crude posts on the other. Several chickens scratched about in the dirt and a few goats and sheep wondered around. A burrow stood tied to a post. A small, unassuming woman stood by an outdoor clay oven removing warm bread. She straightened, turned and faced me. Her manner showed no surprise at my presence. No surprise and definitely no fear. She was dressed in the simple style of a Hebrew peasant woman—a large dark homespun tunic, and a head covering. Over her tunic she wore a full mantle with the front tucked over her girdle to form an apron. What hair that did show revealed a trace of grey. She may have been in her mid to late forties, but her face still held a trace of girlish beauty. I suspected that she had not been overly beautiful even in her youth, pretty but not beautiful. There was a sweetness in her face that I had never seen before. In her dark eyes there rested peace of mind I had not thought possible. And there was something else; there was love there in those eyes, and that face. It was a love I felt more than saw. She placed the bread down on a small board. I stepped down into the glare of the courtyard.

"Do not be afraid," I told her, not knowing why I did. "I am Tribune Claudius Maximus. I was told I could find someone here. I am looking for a woman named Mary."

She smiled a sweet smile. "My name is Mary," she stated.

"No," I said almost apologetically. "The Mary I am looking for is…younger. Her name is Mary Magdalene."

"Mary Magdalene! I know her."

"You do? Is she here?"

"No. I am sorry, she is not."

If Blind Man were here now, I would throttle him.

"Do you know where I can find her?" I asked.

She shook her and said she did not. For some reason I believed her.

I turned to leave, imagining what I would do to Blind Man when I saw him next. The hackles on my neck rose and I turned back to the woman and asked: "How do you know Mary Magdalene?"

"She is a good friend of my son."

I swallowed hard and almost choked on it. I said: "Who is your son?"

A poignant sadness came over her face, and she stated: "My son's name is Jesus."

For a moment I could not move, I could not even speak. I took back half the terrible things I was thinking about Blind Man. After I regained some of my composure, I approached the woman.

"It is of your son that I wish to speak," I managed to say.

She turned away from me and said with some bitterness: "My son was crucified by the Romans, Tribune. Please let him be."

"I am not the only one who will not let him be, woman" I remarked. Her face betrayed nothing. "Your son's body is missing from its tomb." Her face betrayed nothing. "You do not appear surprised at this," I said to her.

Mary turned from me again and brought the bread into the house. I followed her.

"Do you live here?" I asked her in a friendly manner.

"No," Mary replied as she continued with her chores. "My home is in Nazareth. This farm belongs to friends of mine. I stay with them whenever I come to Jerusalem."

"You were present at your son's crucifixion," I said, more of a statement than question. She nodded and I said: "You did not petition the Governor to spare your son's life." She shook her head and I asked: "Why not?"

"It was not up to the Governor," she commented.

"You blame your own people, then?"

"Neither my people nor yours had any control over this matter," she said cryptically.

Frustrated with her replies, I asked: "Where is your husband, woman? I would speak with him."

"My husband died years ago," Mary spoke sadly.

"Then you are alone, with no one to provide for you. Rome took your son and your own people did nothing to prevent it. Are you not at all upset over your son's death?"

She turned to me and looked me in the eye. "My son's death was preordained," she said and meant it. "It had to end like this."

This made less sense, and I began to doubt the woman's sanity. Perhaps she was *non compos mentis.*

Mary left the kitchen and I followed her outside to the far end of the porch where a loom was set up. Woven fabric hung from a crossbeam to another cross-piece where lengths of different coloured yarn hung close to the ground, kept taught by stones and clay weights. She proceeded to weave material as we spoke.

"You may find this difficult to believe, Tribune," Mary spoke calmly, "but my son is the Messiah, the Son of God." I said nothing. It did not escape my notice that she continued to speak of her son in the present tense. That in itself was very interesting.

"How do you know your son is the Son of God?" I asked.

"An angel told me so."

"An angel," I repeated skeptically.

"Yes. Years ago, when I was a very young woman, an angel of the Lord appeared to me and said the Lord was with me, and that I was a woman blessed. The angel said that because I had found favour with God, my womb shall conceive and bring forth a son. His name shall be Jesus, and his kingdom shall have no end." She regarded me closely, smiled that sweet smile and said: "I am not surprised you do not believe me, Tribune."

"I have not said that I do not believe you."

"I can read it on your face," Mary remarked, and she reached over and gently cupped my cheek. "There are some who will not believe even when the proof is before their eyes."

"So far I have seen no proof," I stated.

Mary took her hand from my face and resumed her work, then said: "When my son was a boy, we journeyed from our home in Nazareth to Jerusalem for Passover. At the end of the festival we started back for Nazareth with a caravan. After a day, my husband and I discovered Jesus was not among the caravan. Frantic, my husband and I returned to Jerusalem to search for him. After searching almost the entire city we finally found Jesus in the Temple, sitting among the teachers, talking with them and asking them questions. The teachers were amazed that one so young could speak so learnedly. I was relieved to have found him, but could not help rebuke him, and said: 'Son, why have you treated us so? Behold, your father and I have been looking for you anxiously.' Jesus turned to me and said: 'How is it that you sought me? Did you not know that I must be in my Father's house?'"

"It sounds that even at a young age he was a handful," I commented. "If I had spoken to my parents thus, I might still be wearing the marks of that day."

"It was not precociousness on his part," Mary said knowingly. "He was simply making us aware that he had discovered his life's mission."

I shook my head confused.

"A short number of years ago," Mary continued, "we were attending a marriage in Cana. Halfway through the celebration the bridegroom ran out of wine for his guests. I told my son of our host's dilemma, but Jesus showed no concern. 'Woman,' he said to me, 'what have I to do with it? My hour has not yet come.' Regardless, I called some servants to come over and told them to carry out whatever my son instructed them to do."

"What did he tell them to do?"

"Jesus had them fill six stone jars with water."

"I do not understand," I stated. "Was it some type of jest?"

"Later, when they drew from the jars, they discovered the jars contained wine, a very excellent wine."

"I still do not understand," I said. "Was it a trick of sorts?"

"It was a miracle," she replied. "The first of many."

I regarded her closely looking for any sign of deception or derangement. I saw none. The woman appeared sincere.

"That is all well and good," I told her. "But my problem remains that your son's body is missing from its resting place. Now I am fairly certain his friends—his disciples—have taken the body. I am trying to find them in hopes of finding the body, and lay this entire matter to rest."

"They did not take my son's body from the tomb," she spoke.

"If they didn't; who did?" I asked.

"No one took the body."

"But it is missing."

"His body was not taken," she told me with the confidence of certainty. "He has been resurrected."

Clearly standing before me was a *mater dolorosa*, but I had no time for a woman who was so distraught over her son's death that she had grown delusional.

"Can you tell me where I may find your son's friends?" I asked hoping to get something out of this encounter.

"No," she said simply.

"Do you know if any of them are still in Jerusalem?"

Again she shook her head apologetically. I would have pitied the woman, but she did not appear as if she needed any.

C H A P T E R XIV

▼

A mother's love is a powerful thing. When it comes to her own child, a mother may overlook a myriad of faults out of love for that child. The trouble is, overlooking the faults of a loved one can be a dangerous habit with tragic results.

Take Mary, the mother of Jesus; she had genuine love for her son, and grandiose ideas that he would become a great and powerful person—the son of God, in fact.

Since I was a boy I grew up believing the greatest and most powerful person who ever lived—besides my father—was Gaius Julius Caesar. From a young age I came to revere Gaius Julius Caesar as our nation's most renowned statesman, orator, and military leader. He brilliantly defeated his enemies, both domestic and foreign, and made himself supreme ruler. He even erected a statue of himself bearing the inscription *deo invicto*—to the unvanquished god. The statue claimed Julius Caesar's deification, and that same year a half dozen senators decided to put Caesar's claim to the test. Each senator plunged a dagger repeatedly into the man-god to see if he would bleed. Since then, we Romans have been leery of men proclaiming to be gods.

Prior to seeing the high priest, Joseph Caiaphas, I decided to visit Antonia Fortress to look into the disappearance of the centurion, Lucius Drusus. The Praetor, Servanus, told me the centurion had disappeared without a trace, and I was curious about it. Flavius would tell me if he knew anything, but I could not find him or his companions, Marius, Scarus and Titus.

It was after lunch but I was able to get a late meal at the Fortress before heading off to see Caiaphas. I suspected he would be holding services at the Temple.

The Temple Mount was built by Herod the Great. Construction began about fifty years ago and the old man never lived to see its completion. In fact construction was still going on and would for many years to come. More than once I had walked the walls of the Temple Mount and counted my steps. The south wall was approximately 280 steps, the north wall 315 steps, the east wall 470 steps and the west wall 485 steps.

From the northwest corner of the Temple Mount I entered the Court of the Gentiles, a large open court enclosed by colonnaded porticoes lined with hundreds of huge pillars of white marble. Here in the porticoes were the money changers, who, for a price, would change local and foreign currency into Tyrian shekels, the only currency accepted for offerings in the Temple. Here also were merchants selling small birds and animals to visitors who wished to make a Temple sacrifice. Because of the Passover festival, there were plenty of Jews, both residents of Jerusalem and from foreign countries, who congregated in the court. Here in the Court of the Gentiles, non-Jews were permitted to come and make a sacrifice of their own, or simply admire the architectural marvel of the Temple Mount. In the centre of the court stood the mighty and mysterious Temple, into which no gentile, could enter under penalty of death. Upon my arrival in Jerusalem I was immediately instructed never, under any circumstances, to enter the Temple, for if I did even the Emperor himself could not save me from the death sentence. There were more than a few tales circulating around the Fortress about Romans who had disregarded the warning on the walls of the Temple. The warning was inscribed in Greek and Latin and read:

No foreigner may enter within the balustrade and enclosure around the Temple area. Anyone caught doing so will bear the responsibility for his own ensuing death.

Inside the Temple—I was told by reliable sources—were several chambers. And, I was also told, the further one went into the Temple, the more mysterious it became. Past a stone balustrade and up a low flight of steps was the Court of the Women, so named because this was as far as Jewish women were allowed into the Temple. There inside the Court of the Women, on the west wall, were fifteen curved steps that led to Nicanor Gate and the Court of the Israelites, a long and narrow strip of stone pavement. Past this was the Court of the Priests. In it sat a rough stone alter where bloody animal sacrifices were made. Past here, accessible only to the priests, was the inner sanctuary that housed vessels and furniture made of gold. Finally, the most mysterious of all sanctuaries, a room enclosed from all outside light, a room not barred by mighty doors of metal or wood, but whose entrance was covered by two curtains. Here was the Holy of Holies, a room reserved specifically for the high priest alone, and he only entered it one day a year to stand in God's presence.

In the Court of Gentiles, I instructed a Temple guard, an intelligent looking Levite, that I wished to speak to Joseph Caiaphas, the high priest. He regarded me contemptuously and informed me that the high priest was busy inside the Temple. I told the Levite, in no uncertain terms, that it was important that I see him. The Levite went inside the Temple and returned a short time later saying Caiaphas could not see me now, and, not that I would understand, but this was an important and busy time for the high priest. A bit irate at being rebuffed, I told the Levite that if Caiaphas did not come out to see me, I was going in. The Levite turned his head towards the inscripted warning upon the Temple wall and invited me to do so. I decided to wait outside. It was a long wait. The bright sun of midday had turned from white to yellow by the time I was informed that Caiaphas would see me, and that I was to wait in the Royal Portico just south of the Temple.

Like most of Jerusalem's high priests, Joseph Caiaphas came from the wealthy class, and a high priestly family. He had been high priest for the last eleven years. It had not hurt his position any to marry the daughter of Annas, the previous high priest, who had held the position for nine years. Both lived in fine homes in the southeast section of the Upper City. It was reassuring to know that nepotism was not limited to Romans.

The sun was sinking low in the western sky when Joseph Caiaphas arrived at the Royal Portico to meet with me. He was dressed in a blue robe worn over a white tunic. The blue robe, fringed with golden bells and pomegranates, distinguished him from the other temple priests who wore plain white ankle-length tunics. Over his tunic he wore something like a vest embroidered with bands of gold, purple, scarlet and blue tied at the waist. Upon his chest was a square gold purse set with twelve gemstones. Upon his head Caiaphas wore a headdress of blue, white and gold. He was not a tall man, and though he may have been approximately forty years of age, his face was stern with worry and responsibility. He wore his dark hair shorter than most of his ilk, and his face was covered with a mustache and full beard. Why these Hebrews insisted on beards was beyond comprehension. No self-respecting Roman would have hair on his face. It was not civilized. The high priest and I had never met and we exchanged introductions and a few light amenities.

"It is not permitted that I speak with you, Tribune," said Joseph Caiaphas.

"I understand that," I told him. "I will try not to keep you too long. I am looking into the missing body of the Nazarene, Jesus, from his tomb. It has come to my attention that you know something of this matter."

Caiaphas looked at me trying not to reveal his discomfort that I knew he was in some way connected with the affair.

"What I know, Tribune, is very little," he spoke with false modesty. "I do not know how I may help you."

"You are the head of the Sanhedrin," I said and he nodded. "Jesus was brought before the tribunal for questioning. You sent him to Pontius Pilate and insisted that Jesus was a dissident. After his crucifixion you requested Roman guards be posted at the tomb of Jesus."

Caiaphas raised his heavy, dark eyebrows and regarded me with some surprise. "My dear Tribune, you do seem quite knowledgeable regarding events that do not involve you."

"It is my duty to be knowledgeable regarding events that do not involve me," I said. "Do you deny any of the statements which I just made?"

"By no means," he replied. "Everything you said is true, though with no concept of my people or how we conduct our society, you may have drawn incorrect conclusions from your inferences."

"Oh, and what might those be?"

Caiaphas forced a grin and said: "I, too, must confess to being ignorant regarding the workings of the Roman mind."

"I believe you understand me perfectly."

"You do me honour," he said. "As to questioning Jesus; as the high priest it is my sacred duty to seek out and expose blasphemers, those who speak out against the word of God. Word had reached the Sanhedrin regarding Jesus and his unorthodox teachings. We needed to clarify some important points with him, and so Jesus was brought before the elders and scribes. Witnesses came forth and testified against him. One witness actually stated that Jesus said he would destroy the Temple of God and build it in three days. This disturbed us greatly, for you must know that as a people we honour the Temple above all else. As grievous as this was, there was something even more blasphemous. It had come to our attention that Jesus had made certain claims of the most serious nature."

"What was his claim?"

Caiaphas looked at me and endeavoured to appear very stern and serious. "The man Jesus, it was related to us, claimed to be the Christ, the Son of God."

"And?"

"And so we asked him. We put the question to him if he were the Christ, the Son of God."

"And what did he say?"

"Jesus replied that if he told us, we would not believe."

Somewhere in the back of my mind that statement seemed very familiar.

"What did you do then?" I asked.

"We repeated the question"

"Did he answer you?"

"Yes," Caiaphas said slowly. "Let me put it to you exactly the way Jesus did. When asked if he were the Son of God, Jesus said: 'I am; and you will see the Son of man seated at the right hand of Power, and coming with the clouds of heaven.'"

I gave Caiaphas a questioning look and he explained.

"To us the meaning was clear," the high priest said. "When Jesus said 'Power' he was referring to God. He was claiming his divinity. It was a clear admission of blasphemy. Our laws state the man's words warranted death. Since only the Roman governor could condemn a man to death, Jesus was brought before Pontius Pilate."

"I spoke with the Governor," I stated. "Pilate told me that when he questioned Jesus he could find no guilt in the man. Pilate wanted to release Jesus, but you and your elders pressed him to put Jesus to death."

"You must understand," he said slowly and deliberately. "It is our way. It is our law. Beside, the only reason Pilate wished to release the man is that it was the opposite of what we desired. Your Governor is notorious for such behaviour. There is little love between us, and he would do anything to undermine my authority."

"Allow me to be perfectly honest," I began.

"That would prove refreshing for a Roman," Caiaphas interjected, and I continued.

"Why you wanted Jesus out of the way is entirely your concern. Believe me, I have seen more political intrigue in Rome than you could ever imagine. I do not care why you wanted the man dealt with. I do not even care if he was guilty of anything. The man's life and manner of death do not concern me overly. I am interested only in what became of his body after his death. And in regards to his dead body; why did you arrange to have guards, and Roman guards in particular, posted at the tomb of Jesus? Why, when these same Roman guards came and told you of an incredible story that took place at the tomb, did you instruct them to relate the entirely false story of Jesus's followers coming in the night to steal away the body? And why, to seal the pact, did you give them money?"

I was waiting to drop this one on him. Ever since the night Flavius confessed it to me, I had looked forward to using it. What would Caiaphas say? How would he talk his way out of this? I stood waiting for him to stumble and trip over his own words.

"Tell me, Tribune, is this your first visit to the Temple?" Caiaphas asked me in a friendly fashion. He gestured to the building in the centre of the court. "It is quite magnificent, is it not? This Temple is actually the third Temple to sit upon the Mount. The first Temple, envisioned by King David and built by his son, Solomon, stood for four hundred years and was destroyed by the Babylonians about six hundred years ago. The second Temple lasted for almost five hundred years to be replaced by this one. It is the heart of our faith. Hebrews from all over the world pay tithes to the Temple. Even in Rome you build temples to your gods to honour them. Here is where our God abides. On a visit to Jerusalem your own countryman, Marcus Agrippa, once sacrificed one hundred oxen as a burnt offering. After laying siege to the city and capturing Jerusalem, your great general, Pompey, was driven by curiosity to see inside the Temple. Do you know the story, Tribune? Pompey killed anyone who stood in his way, so he might enter the Temple. And once he had done so, he allowed what priests who survived the slaughter to purify the sanctuary after his desecration.

"As a people we have been delivered from slavery at the hands of the Egyptians, and the Babylonians. We have conquered and been conquered, yet we survive, and our people will continue to survive. You may occupy our land, but you may never occupy our hearts and minds. Neither the Romans, nor Greeks, nor any nation can ever totally destroy us, for our God, the one true God, is with us, and He may never be destroyed, so we may never be destroyed."

This was not going exactly as I imagined.

"You can hide behind all the history you want," I told him. "You may claim that God is on your side, Caiaphas, but from where I stand, you and your people are the same as anyone else. And as for your Temple, it may stand for a thousand years to come, or it could be destroyed tomorrow. Moses may have had the ear of God, but from what I can see, you are not Moses. You may think that as high priest you are exempt from my questions, but that is not the case. Neither you nor I are leaving here until I am satisfied. I hope I make myself clear."

"Perfectly," Caiaphas spoke as if spitting out each syllable. "I am well versed with Roman bullying. Now, ask your questions."

"Why did you pay the Roman guards to change their story about what occurred at the tomb of Jesus?"

"I did not pay them to do anything."

"When they came to you and told you what happened, you paid them!" I insisted.

"When they came and told me what happened I did not pay them," he reiterated. "Why would I pay the guards for falling asleep and allowing someone to come and take the body of the Nazarene?"

"That is not what happened," I said.

"That is what they told me happened," the high priest remarked. "What did they tell you?" he asked smugly. I could have struck the man for his smugness. There seemed no way to get him to change his story other than beating it out of him.

"Now, Tribune, if you will excuse me, this encounter has left me soiled. I feel I must immerse myself in the *mikveh* before I can return to my duties."

Caiaphas turned to leave and I blurted out: "I suppose you deny you paid Judas Iscariot?"

The high priest stopped abruptly, and turned to face me.

"I do not deny it," Caiaphas uttered a little uneasily. "Judas Iscariot came to us and performed a service, and he was paid."

"Thirty pieces of silver is good payment," I remarked with a touch of sarcasm. "It must have been some service."

"Let us not play games, Tribune. The man Iscariot came to us. We did not seek him out."

"And what was the reason he came to you?"

Caiaphas let out a breath through his nostrils. He turned and faced the Temple as if to derive strength from the building. "As the high priest my duties are many. One of the most important of my duties is to see that our people obey the law. My fellow priests and I are watch-keepers of the law, seeing that our people do not transgress from the high moral structure which has taken us thousands of years to achieve as a nation. The man Iscariot came to us to report such a breach of the law—our law, Tribune, not yours."

"And thirty pieces of silver is the price for turning in a man who has broken your law," I said.

"The money was returned."

"Judas Iscariot gave the money back?" I asked, somewhat surprised.

Caiaphas did not appear at all comfortable discussing it. "Yes," he uttered. "Iscariot came back to us somewhat distressed and returned the money."

"Did he say why?"

"It appeared that he regretted his original decision."

"And now he is dead," I stated plainly.

"Regrettable, but true."

"How did he die?" I asked.

Caiaphas paused. "It is my understanding that he took his own life. As a Roman, you should fully appreciate his actions."

"Why would he kill himself?"

"Who may say what is in another man's heart or mind?"

"Perhaps he felt tortured after he betrayed his friend, and could not live with what he had done."

Caiaphas said nothing.

"Would you care to hear what I was told regarding what occurred at the tomb of Jesus?" I asked, but still he said nothing. "I was told that the ground shook, the rock covering the tomb rolled away and there was a blinding light. The guards were struck down and could not move. Later when they could stand, they found the tomb empty. Now does that sound like something Jesus's followers could do?"

Still Caiaphas said nothing. After a tense silence he asked: "Just what is it you want of me, Tribune?"

"I have already said: I am attempting to find the missing body of Jesus."

"I do not know where it is."

"You may not, but to find the body of a dead man I must learn something about his life and the circumstances of his death. Of that, I am certain, you do know something. I know you and Pontius Pilate are stealing money from the Temple treasury. And if the two of you were in that together, it is not difficult to imagine that you both conspired in the death of Jesus—that the two of you pledged to act *coniunctis viribus*. Do you know what that means? That with united powers you sought his death. Though you will not admit it, I know you were informed of what happened at the tomb and that you paid the guards to give false witness about it. I also know of your servant who was in the garden of Gethsemane when Jesus was arrested. Your servant was struck on the ear and Jesus healed him. I am going to find that servant, and when I do…"

My last sentence trailed off, Caiaphas was smiling down at me, a self-righteous type of smile. I did not like it on him.

"Why are you smiling?" I asked.

"I was simply thinking, Tribune. Do you know what a scapegoat is?"

"A what?"

"A scapegoat." He looked at me and I shook my head. "Allow me to explain," he said. "In the month of Tishri, during Yom Kippur, we fast for one day, and that day we call the Day of Atonement. It is an important day, a solemn day. That is the time when, as high priest, it is my sacred duty to go before the Lord and offer atonement for the sins of our nation. The Day of Atonement is a very busy time for me. Seven days prior to it I enter a special room to prepare. Great care is taken in preparation for that day. Every ritual is carefully studied and executed to the last detail. When the day finally arrives, I wear special vestments and preside over all Temple services. It is the one day of the year I am permitted to enter the Holy of Holies. Three times I go into the sacred room. First to make an offering of incense. The second time I sprinkle the blood of a young bull that was sacrificed earlier as an offering for my sins and the sins of all the priests. Later, two goats are chosen. One is to be offered as a burnt sacrifice. The third and final time I enter the room, that goat's blood is sprinkled about. Before I do this, however, a second goat—the scapegoat—is brought before the altar. This goat has a more ominous role. By the altar I lay my hands upon the scapegoat and make a confession for all the people, and their collective sins are placed upon the goat. Afterwards a priest leads the animal into the deadly Judean Wilderness, and it is cast over a cliff. When the scapegoat goes off the precipice, so also go all the sins placed upon it, and in this way we atone for the sins of the Jewish people, both wilful and unintentional.

"In many ways, Tribune, you remind me of the scapegoat. Your people send you out to atone for the sins of your Empire. They enslave and conquer, steal by taxation, rape entire nations, murder and covet, impose their will upon others, and with that done, they feast and drink to celebrate and reward themselves for being great leaders, and statesmen, and philosophers. But when things begin to go awry, when their own sins begin to unravel the glorious tapestry their pride has woven, they call on you in an attempt to make sense of it all, to take the loose threads and make them into something other than what they are. Rome orders you to take their sins and make something noble out of them, and to blame others for what has occurred. They want you to take truth and corrupt it into something obscene, something the Roman mind can understand. The Roman conscience cannot live with what it has done, so all their guilt and sinfulness are placed on you, and you are thrown over the cliff of decency into an abyss of damnation from which your soul cannot escape. Rome cares no more for you than we do for the scapegoat. You are simply something to be used and discarded. You are expendable. You are nothing in their eyes."

I was not certain, but I did not think it was a compliment.

"When your Day of Atonement comes, Caiaphas, be certain to recall the sins you committed today. I believe lying is one of them."

He smiled a weak smile and said: "You know, Tribune, there is an old Hebrew saying that translates into something like this: 'It is easier to speak with a deaf man, than it is to a man with the mind of an ass.'"

I was not certain, but I did not think it was a compliment.

"In Rome we have a few old sayings of our own," I told him. "*Mentulam caco!*"

It was not a compliment.

CHAPTER XV

▼

I left Caiaphas standing in the Royal Portico staring at me, his mouth hanging open. He obviously was not used to being insulted in Latin.

Back at Antonia Fortress I hoped to find out something about the missing centurion, Lucius Drusus. I was unable to discover anything regarding the centurion from his superiors, so I decided to see if I could learn anything from the men under his command. I did not find young Flavius, but did manage to track down two of his comrades, Titus and Scarus. They eyed me suspiciously during our talk, and their manner was cold in the extreme. When asked the whereabouts of their companions Marius and Flavius, they told me the two had volunteered for extra patrol duty. They also told me that Drusus simply could not be found one day, and no one seemed to have any idea where he was or what had become of him. He had simply disappeared, leaving no trace except the centurion uniform left in his quarters. Neither of them appeared overly concerned about their superior's absence. The centurion's disappearance both interested and disturbed me, but I could devote no more time to it, and would leave it for the nonce.

The meeting with Caiaphas had not gone as well as I had hoped and it preyed on my mind. There were several things I had to think over. I decided to pay a visit to Marcus Malachi.

I arrived at the home of my friend and found him in an agreeable mood. Marcus told me he was just about to eat dinner. I proceeded to excuse myself, but he invited me to stay and break bread with him. I asked him if he were afraid of someone seeing us eat together, but he only uttered a strange word, and told me not to worry. The table was set and all his servants had left the house for the evening. I followed him into a simple room where a low table was set with bowls and platters of food. There were dishes of lamb, cheese, unleavened bread, wine, nuts, a few vegetables, and fruit. The food was served in common bowls. Marcus washed his hands before we began, and I followed his example.

Over dinner Marcus asked me how my investigation was progressing. I filled him in on all my findings so far, from my meeting with Joseph and Nicodemus at the tomb, to my interviews with Lucius Drusus, and the four Roman guards and their assault upon me. I told him of how I got Flavius to confess to the attack, and that he revealed to me what actually had occurred at the tomb. Marcus seemed very interested in my interviews with Pontius Pilate and Herod Antipas. He was curious regarding my talk with Mary, the mother of Jesus. Lastly, I told Marcus of my talk with the High Priest, Joseph Caiaphas.

"He compared me to a goat," I said.

"A goat?" Marcus repeated.

"Yes. A scapegoat."

Marcus tried not to smile, but there was a definite gleam in his eyes.

"But you could not get him to confirm the young guard's story," Marcus said, trying to get his mind off some bizarre mental image he was forming, presumably of me with a set of horns and a tuft of beard.

"The man would rather die than admit the guards even confessed the story to him," I said with frustration. "Why would Caiaphas be afraid to repeat the guard's account?"

Marcus thought a moment, and said: "If the high priest were to repeat it, he would, in essence, be giving credence to the fact that Jesus may be divine. In his position Caiaphas could not afford to do that."

"If I could only get hold of his servant who received the wound in the garden the night they arrested Jesus," I said hopefully.

Marcus shook his head. "If I know Caiaphas, he most certainly has the man hid away some place where you will never find him. The servant is most likely out of the city by this time."

"I wish I might have spoken with Judas Iscariot before he died," I remarked.

"Can you find no one who knew him?"

"The only ones who knew him well are his fellow disciples, and they are all in hiding. And now the centurion in charge of the crucifixion is missing. Somehow I must get the other three guards to confirm the story Flavius told me about the morning at the tomb."

"Will they confirm it?"

"Most likely not, but I must try. I am running out of options."

Marcus stared at me contemplatively. He sat back from the table, chewed, swallowed and smacked his lips. "There may be one option you have yet to consider," he said to me, as he filled my wine cup.

"And what might that be?"

Marcus paused and stared at me intently. "Let us drink first," he said.

We raised our cups and drank deep. Marcus resumed staring at me. He leaned closer and said in a hushed tone: "Have you considered that perhaps Jesus was exactly what he claimed to be, and that he did indeed rise from the dead?"

Now it was my turn to stare. "Have you lost your mind?" I asked him.

Marcus did not answer, but asked again: "Have you considered it?"

"No."

"Why not?" he said. "Some of the evidence clearly points in that direction. Why have you not considered it?"

"Because it is so ridiculous!"

"Why?"

"Why! Why! What would be the point? If Jesus were your Messiah, why die on the cross? Why not call on a holy host of angels to come and destroy the entire Roman Legion? What would be the point of rising from the dead?"

Marcus reached over with a hand and tapped my forehead with his finger.

"You are closing your mind to possibilities, young Claudius," he told me in his tutorial attitude. "You must learn to think with an open mind. Do not ask *why* he would do it. Simply ask *if* he could do it. If Jesus were the Son of God, could he do it?"

"Yes," I answered somewhat reluctantly. "I suppose if Jesus were the son of your God he could do it."

"Then why have you not considered it?"

"I do not know," I admitted feebly. "Perhaps I was afraid to consider it."

"Now, that is an honest answer," Marcus said to me consolingly. "And honesty is always in demand, but often in short supply."

"My head aches," I said. "I do believe I drank too much. Maybe I need to immerse myself in the *mikveh*."

"The *mikveh*?" Marcus repeated confused.

"It was something Caiaphas had said," I told him. "Marcus, what is the *mikveh*?"

"It is a ritual bath cut into stone. You must have seen them. There is a public one near the Temple Mount for worshippers to use before entering holy ground. The bath is more for cleansing the spirit rather than the body. There are several *mikveys* in the Temple, two reserved for the high priest himself."

"It sounds wonderful," I commented and thought how enjoyable a nice cool bath would feel.

Marcus Malachi nodded and said, "It is not so different from Roman baths."

"You know, it is strange," I said, pouring myself another cup of wine. "Both Herod and Caiaphas made it clear to me that it was Rome that condemned Jesus, and that he died by Roman decree. They wanted no responsibility for his death. Caiaphas even said that Jesus was brought before Pilate because the Governor was the only one who had the authority to condemn a man to death."

"That is not entirely true," Marcus remarked casually.

"What do you mean?"

"The Sanhedrin can pronounce a death sentence upon a blasphemer. The guilty may be strangled outside the city or stoned to death."

"If the Sanhedrin had the authority," I said somewhat bewildered, "then why did they not simply execute Jesus themselves? Come to think of it, even Herod could have had Jesus put to death. He did as much for a man named John the Baptist. Why would they need Rome to execute the man?"

Marcus shook his head. "I never thought about it," he uttered.

"Unless," I said as my brain slowly began to work through the wine. "Unless they did suspect Jesus was something like he claimed to be, and the chief priests and elders feared him enough to want to be rid of him, but feared him too much to do it themselves."

"Now you are thinking with an open mind," Marcus said smiling proudly.

We talked long into the night. The hour was well past sundown when I left the house of Marcus Malachi, and darkness covered my departure. The Jerusalem nights were not as hot as the days and I almost enjoyed the evening. I considered stopping at the barracks to see if Flavius had returned from patrol, before I returned to my quarters.

It was not long before I imagined someone was following me. It was not much longer before I was certain of it. I did not turn around or in any way reveal to my pursuer that I knew of his presence. I turned down a dark street and hid in the recess of a doorway. Soon the sound of footsteps reached me. They drew closer and I placed my hand inside my tunic to feel for my knife. It was not there. I must have misplaced it somewhere.

The night held few stars, but there was enough starlight to cast a dim shadow. The shadow crept across the ground. I braced myself. The figure of a man loomed before me and I lunged, throwing all my weight upon him. With a keening cry the man pitched back as I fell upon him, and we both hit the ground. Scrambling atop the man, I wrapped my hands around his throat.

"Tell me why I should not kill you now!" I grunted.

A feeble, choking cry emitted from his lips. It was a familiar feeble, choking cry. I released my grip slightly.

"Maximus, don't kill me!"

"Jupiter! Blind Man!" I exclaimed. "I told you never to do that again!"

I released my grip upon his throat, rolled off him and dragged him to his feet.

"One day," I uttered, "you are going to wind up with a knife in your belly and wonder why."

"Did you ever stop to consider you simply might be a bit too nervous?" Blind Man snapped back at me.

"What do you want?"

"I found Mary," he said.

"Another one? That last one was not even the Mary I wanted."

"You said a woman named Mary who knew Jesus," he argued. "You were not that particular."

"I want Mary Magdalene!"

"I found Mary Magdalene," he said. "Or, at least, she has been seen."

"Where?" I said.

Of all the people who had known Jesus, or had been close to him, the name Mary Magdalene came up more than any other, even that of his mother. According to most of my sources, Mary Magdalene was a Galilean, a known prostitute, and a follower of Jesus. She was seen at his crucifixion, and present when he was buried. She was also present at his tomb on the day of his so-called resurrection. Magdalene was also reported to have both seen and talked with Jesus after his death and burial. If anyone knew where the body of Jesus was taken, it would be Mary Magdalene.

Blind Man sent me to the Essene Quarter on the south side of Jerusalem. The hour was late and this part of the city looked as black as the inside of a closed tomb. Blind Man was not able to give me the exact location where Magdalene could be found, but he was able to narrow it down to a specific area. I walked the deserted streets slowly, keeping to the shadows, and making as little noise as possible. Whenever I heard a sound or detected any movement I stopped instantly and made myself part of a wall or doorway.

It was a long wait, and I passed the time by mulling over the problem at hand. As Marcus Malachi had suggested, I attempted to keep an open mind to the entire affair. So I proposed the theory: Could the man, Jesus have survived the crucifixion? It was an idea I had considered earlier. I was convinced that the missing centurion was connected in some way. Even his own men admitted that

Drusus had been acting strangely since the crucifixion of Jesus. But why? There was a very good chance that the centurion was involved much more than I originally suspected. He more than likely was in league with Jesus's followers and perhaps that was the reason he did not have Jesus's legs broken as he hung on the cross. Drusus very likely arranged to have the Nazarene's still living body taken down and given to Joseph of Arimathea so they might have an opportunity to heal the man's wounds in some safe and secluded location. It would have been simple enough to make a switch and place another body in the tomb, then come back and steal it away. Lucius Drusus may have fled for he feared I might soon discover the conspiracy. Truth be known, the disciples may have killed the centurion to keep him from ever telling what he knew. It was very likely they had done the same to Judas Iscariot. People said he had killed himself, but he may have been murdered and made to look like suicide. Iscariot must have known something regarding Jesus's death. Perhaps he knew that Jesus was not even dead! Perhaps Iscariot discovered the deception, objected to it and was killed to keep him from revealing the truth.

And what of the guard's strange story? Might not have the wine they drank been drugged to paralyse them, and they only imagined the bright light at the tomb? Then there were the three major characters in the drama, namely Pilate, Caiaphas and Herod. What were they hiding? I could not help but suspect a *consensus audacium*—an agreement of rash men. But who conspired with whom? Were all three in it together? What did they hope to gain? My mind began to spin on it all.

It was very late and I was forced to pinch myself just to stay awake. Dawn would break in a little while, and I hoped Mary Magdalene would show herself before long. As if in answer to my hopes, I heard the light sound of leather sandals on dirt. I stopped where I was and stood perfectly still, half in shadow and half in moonlight. Carefully, I peered in the direction of the sound. At first I thought my ears were playing tricks. Nothing moved and no further sound came forth. I stood there barely breathing, my eyes straining through the darkness. After several tense moments I saw it—movement at the far end of the street. Something moved as the night itself—slow and silent. I could just make it out now. The lithe figure of a woman, stealthily gliding down the street, her form cloaked and hooded. She appeared to be carrying a bundle in her arms. She moved towards me. If she peered far enough ahead, she would see me, but I was reluctant to step deeper into the shadows lest she detect my movement and flee the scene. I remained still and counted on good fortune to work in my favour. She continued to move towards me. I was holding my breath now. She stopped and I was certain she saw me. The woman cautiously peered around and laid her hand upon the latch of a gate in a wall that surrounded a large, two-storeyed building. Involuntarily, I released the breath I was holding and she stopped. Had she heard it? The sound had been so quiet I could not believe she had heard it, but she raised her head and glanced in my general direction. Slowly she moved away from the door and walked up the street towards me. She stopped before another door, and as before, placed her hand upon it and moved on. The woman crossed the street and repeated this act on several other doors, only now she was moving away from me. Her back was to me now, so I risked taking a step. She must have heard it, for she turned her head towards me and I knew she was ready to flee.

"Halt, in the name of Caesar!" I shouted. I should have known that would be a waste of breath. She dropped her bundle, and fled down the street. I followed in pursuit.

Either the woman was a fast runner, or I was slower than I care to admit. She turned one corner after another, and I did not seem to gain any distance on her. During daylight, I could navigate the steep, hilly streets of Jerusalem fairly well. But in the darkness, the untidy layout of the houses huddled around common courtyards made things confusing and it was difficult to keep my sense of direction. At one point I thought I had lost my quarry, only to discover she was now behind me. I turned in time to see her duck into a dark alley. I was at the alley in a brief moment. My breathing was heavy now, and my heart pounded in my ears. The alley was dark, so dark in fact, that I could not see anything, but could only hear the fleeing footsteps of my quarry. I would certainly lose her if I did not follow her immediately. Oh well, as my old teacher used to tell me; *audaces fortuna iuvat*. I took a breath, and plunged blindly down the alley at a run. I remember a sudden, and dazzling burst of light, followed by the darkness of oblivion.

When I woke, I found myself laying on my back upon the ground. The morning sun illuminated the alley, and I heard sounds of the city as it woke to begin a new day. My head ached. I went to sit up but my head told me not to do that. A groan issued up from my vitals to help fight off the nausea that threatened to overwhelm me. Slowly, I recalled what had occurred. I assumed I was lying in the alley I blundered into hours before. My hand went to my head, and more pain raced into my skull. I gently felt the front of my head that was now swollen from some blow. Mary Magdalene must have been very good, or very lucky to swing something at me in the dark and hit me square in the forehead. I got to my knees, then my feet, pulling myself up with the aid of a wooden beam that stretched across the alley. Some fool had stretched a wooden beam across the alley! And it was just my height. I examined the beam and noticed a mark near the centre of it. I suspected that it matched perfectly with the mark on my forehead. I was tired, my head ached terribly, and I thought I might vomit. *Vulneratus non victus*, I decided it was time to go home.

CHAPTER XVI

▼

I awoke in my bed and instantly realized that there was someone in the room with me. Ignoring my aching head, I bolted upright and groped for my dagger. It was not there.

A man sat in a chair six paces from my bed. The room was dark but I knew he was there, sitting in my chair, staring at me. I could not remember a time when so many uninvited guests entered my quarters.

"Who are you?" I demanded. "What do you want?"

The figure sat very still, dressed in a dusty, hooded cloak. The hood shadowed much of his face and I could not see his features clearly. His manner of dress identified him as a Hebrew. Without a word he raised his hands to his hood and lowered it. I was slightly taken aback. He was a young man, perhaps not twenty years of age. His bright brown eyes, gentle features and light beard lent him a harmless quality that allowed me to relax my suspicions. He was covered with dust, and appeared weary from much travel.

"You are Tribune Claudius Maximus?" he asked in an even tone. His voice was as placid as his appearance.

"I know who I am," I grumbled. "Who in Hades are you?"

"My name is John."

"What do mean by coming here?" I demanded, still sounding angry. "What is it you want?"

"I wanted to see you," he said.

"You wanted to see me regarding what?"

"The others said I should not come," John said, as though I knew of who he spoke. "They thought it is too dangerous for me to come. I felt that I must. Peter did not forbid me to come, but urged me to be wary."

"Wary of what?" I asked. "Who are the others? Who is Peter?"

"You seek Mary Magdalene," he said, more as a statement than a question.

"How do you know that? Do you know her? Do you know where I can find her?"

John nodded. "She has agreed to meet you," he said, then added: "If my encounter with you goes well, I will advise her to meet with you. Both Mary and Peter agreed they would trust my judgement."

"You are one of them, are you not?" I said. "You are one of the disciples of Jesus."

He neither denied nor confirmed my statement, but I knew it to be true.

"There are some questions I need answered," I told him.

He shook his head slowly. "Mary is the one you must talk to," John responded.

"When can I meet her?"

"You will be contacted," he said.

"When? Where?" I asked. I was closer than I had ever been, and there was urgency in my voice.

"You will be contacted," John repeated. "You should rest now."

John rose to leave. I tried to stand up, but the pain in my head suddenly returned, and I fell back onto the bed. I do not remember falling asleep.

It was late afternoon by the time I woke. I put my hand to my forehead and could feel oil. Ruth must have come home and tended to me in my sleep. There was no sign of her now, but she left me a bowl of barley porridge and bread. The porridge was still warm, so she could not have left long ago. I gobbled up the meagre fare and got dressed while I thought about my early morning visitor and all he had said. There was no point in seeking him out. The best thing to do was to trust in what he said and wait to be contacted. Though I searched my quarters, I could not find my dagger. It was as if it had disappeared. I felt naked without it, but I dressed and went out into the heat of the day.

Once outside I realized there was no place to go. I felt my investigation had ground to a halt and I did not know what to do next. I decided to go to the public bath house in hopes of cooling off a mite. While I was there, I fought the urge to drown myself.

I left the bath, somewhat refreshed, and went to the praetorium. I still needed to speak with Flavius and see if he could convince the other three guards to confirm his story of the morning at the tomb. In the barracks, I found no trace of Flavius or any of his comrades. A centurion was passing by and I inquired as to their whereabouts. The centurion donned a strange expression. He could not say where I might find Marius, Scarus and Titus, but he did manage to tell me that young Flavius was dead. I tried not to show my shock and surprise. When I asked how Flavius had died, the centurion told me that Flavius had chosen to fall upon his own sword. When I asked where this occurred, he told me it was when Flavius had been out on patrol duty. I questioned the centurion about Lucius Drusus, but he could tell me nothing.

I left the praetorium thinking about Flavius falling on his sword, and wondered if Marius had given the young soldier any help. Flavius had told me they had all taken an oath on their lives not to tell anyone what had occurred at the tomb. Perhaps Marius had taken the oath seriously, and when he found out Flavius had told me about it, Marius decided to execute the consequence.

With nothing else to do except wait to be contacted by one of the Jesus-ites, I decided to put my time to good use and find Marius to see where that would lead. After a lengthy wait, Marius came out of the praetorium and walked through the market and into the Upper City. There, he went into the theatre near the wall that separated Upper City from Lower City. I thought this peculiar. Marius did not strike me as your typical theatergoer.

Like many buildings in Jerusalem the theatre was built by Herod the Great approximately fifty years ago. The theatre was built in the Roman fashion with the audience sitting on stone steps placed in a half-circle facing the stage. On each side of the stage were two-storey scene buildings complete with doors and balconies for use by the actors during the performance. I obtained a bone token that allowed me entrance, and followed Marius into the theatre. It was a grand structure, by Judean standards, with ornate carvings, marble inlays, and silk fabrics imported from the East. Since the Hebrews did not permit graven images in the city, there were no magnificent statues like the ones that could be found in theatres back in Rome. Instead military trophies were displayed as decorations.

The late afternoon performance was underway. It was a comedy by Menander, who some saw as more subtle and refined than Aristophanes. I preferred the tragedies of Euripides, since I could relate better to them. I followed Marius with my eyes as he circled the audience as if looking for someone. He spotted the person, and made his way towards him. I kept both my distance and Marius's back to me so he would not see me. Marius sat next to a man dressed in a hood and long robe. Try as I may I could not get a good look at the man. They talked for some time. Marius did most of the talking. Something passed between them, then Marius stood up and left.

I began to follow Marius out the south exit of the theatre, then cursed myself for a dolt. Following Marius was less important than finding out with whom he had spoken. I let Marius go his way and turned my attention to his theatre companion. When I looked back to their seats, the stranger was gone. I quickly scanned the theatre for the hooded man, and, for a moment, thought he had eluded me until I saw him leaving out a north exit. I ran around the half-circle of the top step and raced out the same exit. The narrow streets of Jerusalem were crowded and I decided to find a position above the pedestrians so I might get a better view. Much to the protest of a tradesman repairing a house, I climbed his ladder, and, shielding my eyes against the low, late afternoon sun, I looked in every direction. I spotted the man—thank the gods—passing through a gate, heading east. I still could not see his face but recognized the hooded robe he wore. Climbing down the ladder, I started off at a run for the very gate the man passed through. Once there I was plagued with the same problem I faced before, that of finding him among the crowded streets. I searched and searched, and was certain the man had disappeared into the throng. I turned around and around, darting this way and that, but could find no trace of him. A prickly feeling crept up the nape of my neck. I turned my head and raised my vision. There, on the southwest stairs leading up to the Temple Mount, I saw him. I ran to the stairs, and, taking two at a time, I reached the top and entered the Court of the Gentiles. As usual, crowds of people filled the court, but through the masses I saw the man walking towards the Temple. I pushed my way through the crowds and yelled for the man to stop. He did not stop or slow, but continued his way hastily. I wished he would turn so I might catch a look at his features, but he did not. He was going to enter the Temple, and if he did I knew the chase was done, and I had lost.

"Stop!" I yelled. "Someone stop that man!" My hysterics only garnered me strange looks from everyone. No one appeared to understand my intent, and the man entered the Temple.

I rushed the door and two rather large Levites barred my way.

"Let me pass!" I growled as they caught me up by my arms. "I must stop that man!"

"No, Tribune," one of the Levite guards said. "It is forbidden."

"I am on the Emperor's business," I cried. "I must stop that man!"

"You cannot enter, Tribune," the other Levite warned. "You will die if you enter the Temple."

I looked at their faces trying to determine if they were indeed sincere. They may have known who the man was, or perhaps not. They may have been deliberately keeping me from him, or simply stopping me from entering the Temple for my own good. I could not be certain.

I licked my dry lips and took a deep breath. I was winded from the running. When the Levites knew I would not try to enter the Temple, they released their hold upon me, but continued to bar the doorway. I turned away dejectedly. I knew I would never see the man again. Even if I were to watch every door in the Temple I would not know whom to look for. It would be a simple matter for the man to discard his robe and walk right past me.

I walked about the court thinking over this latest episode. The man must have been a Hebrew—I could hardly imagine anyone risking death to get away from me, and surely the guards would have stopped a non-Jew from entering the Temple as they had me. The strange part was that Jews were seldom seen in the theatre. Greek tragedies and Roman comedies did not appeal to their sensibilities. Yet if a Jew wished to meet someone in public and did not want to be seen by other Jews, the theatre was certainly a safe place to meet. If I had to make a guess, I would assume it was Caiaphas that Marius had met. Marius probably told the high priest what Flavius revealed to me, and that he had killed Flavius for the breach of oath. Caiaphas might have given Marius more money—but for what?

"A pair of birds for a sacrifice, Tribune?"

My musing had so enthralled me that I did not even notice a woman approach me in the court and stand nearly in front of me. In her hand she carried a small wooden cage that contained a pair of turtledoves. She held the cage up for me to see.

"Do you wish to buy them to make a sacrifice, Tribune?" she asked.

"Uhm, no," I uttered, not paying her any mind.

"Are you certain?" she persisted. "They would make an excellent sacrifice. They are a fair price."

"I said no." And I turned away from the woman.

"Please, Tribune."

I turned on her angrily. "Are you addle-minded? I said no!"

"Were you not told you would be contacted?" she said in a low voice. "I have come to take you to Mary Magdalene."

I was taken aback by her statement, and was somewhat surprised when she open the small cage and released the turtledoves into the air. We stood for a moment and watched the birds fly into the air and out of sight.

"I thought they were for a sacrifice," I remarked.

She turned to me and smiled. "And so they were."

She led me away and I followed. We left the Temple Mount by way of the western gate that connected to the viaduct. The viaduct was generally used by the Temple priests, so they might reach the Temple without soiling themselves by the streets or by the people on the streets. They seemed to be a very clean sort.

As we walked westward atop the viaduct with the rooftops of cube-shaped buildings on both sides, I could observe my female companion. She was perhaps in her mid-twenties, tall and lithe, with a rare beauty that she did not flaunt nor attempt to enhance in any way. She did not speak and I asked no questions. We continued along the viaduct towards the setting sun. At the end of it we entered a tower, and descended a spiral staircase. We exited the tower and the city. A road took us north along the western wall of Jerusalem and to Calvary where I had been days before. Empty *stipes* with no *patibulums* stuck out of the ground. The woman stopped before a *stipe* and stood staring at it.

"Strange place to meet," I finally said after a long bout of silence.

The woman started as if she forgot I was there, and turned to me.

"Mary Magdalene wished me to bring you here," the woman stated. "You must wait."

"Why did she wish to meet me here?"

"She has her reasons."

"Who are you?" I asked.

"A friend. I was to meet you first, to be certain it was safe."

"You people are certainly a cautious band," I stated.

"These are dangerous times for us," she responded. "Precautions are a necessity."

"How do you know I did not arrange to have a squad of soldiers follow us?" I put to her.

"Did you?"

"No."

"Then we will wait until Mary comes. Why do wish to meet with her?"

"I have some questions to ask her."

"Questions about her Lord, Jesus?"

"Yes Mary, questions about your Lord, Jesus."

She started again, and smiled uneasily.

"Yes," she admitted. "I am Mary Magdalene. How did you know it was I?"

"Last night in the Essene Quarter, it was I who had chased you through the streets. I could not see your face clearly, but I had the chance to observe you, the way you walk, and move and carry yourself. I am generally quite good at noticing these things. It aids me in my duties."

"And what are your duties?" Mary Magdalene asked.

"Presently, I am trying to find your lord, Jesus."

"I do not believe you wish to become a one of his disciples," she commented with a hint of mockery.

"If you and your kind know who I am, know where I live, and knew that I was looking for you, then you must also know why I am looking for the body of your dead lord."

"You say 'dead lord' as if you expect me to refute his death."

"Do you refute it?" I asked her.

"I do not refute his death," Mary Magdalene replied. "I refute that he is dead."

"Perhaps you should tell me your story."

She looked up again at the cross. She walked up to it and laid her hand upon it.

"He died here, you know," Mary stated. "But it did not end here, nor did it begin here. For me, it began in my hometown of Magdala, on the Sea of Galilee, less than a day's journey from Nazareth. One day a man came to our town from Nazareth. He taught the people and healed the sick. There was none so lowly that he would not give of his time. He said he came to save sinners, and there was none who sinned more than I. I need not go into detail about my life, save to say I lacked moral character."

"You were a whore," I stated blatantly.

My statement neither shocked nor embarrassed her.

"Yes," Mary said in response to my remark. "I slept with men, many men. I slept with women and allowed men to watch. I slept with men and women together. I slept with animals. I slept with—"

"I get the idea," I said, interrupting her. I felt shocked and embarrassed.

"At times I wanted desperately to stop," she said, and there was deep emotion in her voice. "At other times I did not wish to stop, but desired only to delve deeper into my own sinful nature. It was as if I were being pulled apart. When Jesus came to Magdala I heard people speak of him. A great and wonderful teacher some called him. I wanted to see him but shame kept me away. I was certain he would not want to see me. One day I felt compelled to seek him out. He was out in the street speaking with people. I must have looked a sight, for I had sunk down deep into wicked sinfulness. When I approached, others regarded me with disgust and hatred, but when I looked at Jesus, he smiled at me. Somehow I knew he would not turn away. He put out his hands and I took them. I fell to my knees and asked him to help me. I do not recall much of what occurred directly after that. Later, I was told by John that seven demons had hold of me, and that Jesus had cast them out. I cannot tell you how different my life became. He had done such wonders, and asked nothing in return."

"You became one of his followers," I remarked. She nodded and I said: "You were present at his crucifixion."

"Yes," Mary said. "It happened here, at this cross."

"Why did he choose to die?" I asked. "If he were the Messiah, if he could perform miracles, why did he choose to die?"

She shook her head and smiled sadly. "It was so he could perform the greatest miracle of all. So that people would know he is the Christ. He sacrificed himself. He chose to die for my sins and for yours. With his death all sins are washed away."

"Like a scapegoat," I muttered under my breath.

"What did you say?"

I ignored her question and said: "Tell me what occurred at the tomb."

She led me away, and together we made the short walk to the tomb where Jesus's body had been placed.

"We brought his body here," Mary Magdalene spoke. "We had to get him into the tomb before nightfall. We wrapped his body in linen and spices, placed him in the tomb, and rolled the rock over the opening. Out here we wept and prayed. When the Sabbath began, we departed. Two days later I returned with another woman."

"For what purpose?"

"We had been rushed trying to prepare the body for burial. We wanted to make certain Jesus's body was properly anointed. As we walked along, we pondered how the two of us would roll the rock aside, since it took several people to put it in place. As we approached the tomb, we saw Roman guards lying down outside the burial place."

"The guards were lying down?" I interjected. "They were not standing?"

She told me they were not, and added: "They appeared to be sleeping."

I asked: "When you reached the tomb, did you feel the ground shake in any way?"

Again she said no, and I urged her to continue.

"When we reached the tomb we found the stone had already been rolled away. We began to fear the body had been stolen. We looked inside the tomb, and our hearts sank. His body was not there."

"The tomb was empty?" I posed it both as a question and statement.

"Not exactly."

"Not exactly? Not exactly? You said his body was not there! Was someone else there?"

She hesitated, then said: "There was a young man in the tomb. I did not recognize him. His countenance was strange, almost impossible to describe. His face was peaceful, yet full of life, and his entire being seemed to exude power, and light. He was dressed in robes of pure white."

"Was it so white that it hurt your eyes?" I asked, recalling Flavius's words.

"No," Mary replied. "In truth, I found I could not look away. Then he spoke. His voice was calm, though it echoed like thunder."

"What did he say?"

"He greeted us, and told us not to be frightened. He bade us to come into the tomb, so we did. 'You are looking for Jesus of Nazareth,' he told us. 'He is not here. See, his body lay there, but he is risen!' The man then told us to go and tell his disciples what had happened."

"There was no bright light emanating from the tomb?" I asked.

"No."

"And you never saw this man before or since?"

"No."

"What did you do then?" I wanted to know.

"My companion was very frightened and ran off," Mary said and added: "I could hardly blame her. I, myself, was trembling with fear and excitement, but I managed to go to find the disciples."

"And where was that?" I asked.

Mary Magdalene regarded me with suspicion. "I cannot tell you that, Tribune. It is a secret place they use for hiding from persecution, and I have promised never to reveal their location. I can tell you that when I ran to tell the disciples the news, they did not believe me. Try as I might I could not convince them. Finally, Peter and James agreed to come and see for themselves. When we arrived at the tomb, everything was as I had seen it, except the guards were no longer there; neither was the strange man in the tomb who had spoken to me. James and Peter saw this, but they appeared confused and frightened, and did not know what to make of it all. Coming to no conclusion, they returned to their secret place."

"What did you do then?"

"I did not know what to do. They left me here alone. I began to doubt all I had seen and heard. I did not know what to think, and I began to cry. Then, from behind me, a voice said, 'Why do you weep?' I answered, 'They have taken away my Lord and I do not know where to find him.' Then the voice called me by name. I turned to look, and to my astonishment there was my Lord, Jesus! I spoke his name and he said, 'Do not be frightened. Go tell my brothers to leave at once for Galilee and I will meet them there."

"Did they go to Galilee?" I asked. Mary nodded and I said more to myself: "That is why I was not able to find them these last few days." Then I asked Mary: "When did they return?"

"Just this morning," she stated. "They have travelled far, and are once again in hiding. When I told them of you and that you were searching for us, they were suspicious. I knew it was you who chased me through the streets last night, and I knew you would find me eventually. I told my brothers I would meet with you. They believe nothing good can come out of speaking with you. I, on the other hand, thought it best that we meet and speak openly of these things. It was agreed that John would see you first and decide if it were safe. I already knew it was. I am a fairly good judge of character."

"But we have never met," I said confused. "How could you know anything of my character?"

"It was not *your* character I judged, Tribune—but Ruth's."

"Ruth!" I ejaculated. "What has she to do with this?"

"Through sources of my own I learned that you were trying to find me. Later I discovered a young Hebrew woman shared your rooms. I followed her one day to the marketplace and struck up a conversation with her. I like Ruth. I understand her. My past life is similar to hers. We spoke mainly of you. She loves you very much. Through Ruth, I came to know what type of man you are, and decided that I would risk meeting you."

Somehow I felt betrayed and a dozen thoughts raced through my mind—not all of them pleasant. I studied the woman who faced me and knew that she, too, was clever and resourceful. I would have never had found her unless she wished to be found, and that realization made me feel angry and a trifle inadequate. I attempted to get back on the subject.

"And Jesus," I asked, "has he never appeared to you again?"

"No," she replied, and there was sadness in her eyes. "But I have heard my Lord has appeared to others—the disciples being some."

"When did he appear to them?"

"That is not for me to tell you, Tribune. If my brothers decide to meet with you, allow them to tell you their tale."

I nodded and said: "What do you know of a missing centurion named Lucius Drusus?"

"I can tell you nothing of him," was her response, but I suspected she was lying.

"Do you know anything regarding a young Roman soldier named Flavius?"

"No. Should I?"

"He was one of the soldiers guarding the tomb that day. He is dead now, and the centurion, Drusus, is missing."

"I must go now, Tribune."

"Where can I reach you if I need to speak with you again?"

"You cannot," Mary Magdalene said as she began to walk away, and then called over her shoulder: "But if you find you must contact me, tell Ruth and she will know how to reach me."

I was tempted to follow her, but I suspected it would avail me naught. I thought over Mary Magdalene's story and how it conflicted with the one Flavius told me. Flavius had said there was an earthquake, yet Mary said not. Flavius had said a blinding white light shone from the direction of the tomb, yet Mary said not. Why would Flavius concoct such details? Why would Mary omit them? Strangely enough, I tended to believe them both. Yet how was that possible? It was difficult to tell whether she was lying about seeing Jesus alive. If he were alive that means he did not die on the cross as told to me. Did she experience a *deceptio visus* and simply imagine seeing him? Or was it just someone who looked like Jesus? Who was the young stranger inside the tomb? He obviously had taken Jesus's corpse. If Jesus were alive, this unknown man might have aided in releasing him from the tomb. But why would he return? And why would he tell Mary to have the disciples leave for Galilee? Perhaps it was to get them out of Jerusalem—but for what purpose? Now the disciples had returned. I needed to speak with them and hear their side of the story. This was getting far too confusing.

CHAPTER XVII

▼

Rome sat at the very heart of her Empire that reached to Britain in the north, Cyrene on the coast of Africa, Cadiz in Spain and Jerusalem in the eastern provinces. Trade routes were the grease on the axil of the great Roman machine that kept the wheels moving. Every port on the Mediterranean Sea imported and exported goods from Rome. Grain from Egypt, wine from Gaul, timber from Macedonia and balm from Arabia all found their way to Rome. Even beyond the Empire goods travelled overland and by sea from India and China. All of this trade was made possible by Roman law and order which kept the peace, and by the excellent road system the Roman engineering corps provided. 'All roads lead to Rome', was a phrase known throughout the Empire. The roads were originally constructed for the Roman army and Roman officials, but this did not keep locals from using them.

In the eastern provinces, like Judea, roads were used by travellers, but were fundamental trade routes for commerce. Trade caravans constantly passed through Jerusalem from Palmyra to the north, Petra to the south, Alexandria to the west, and as far as Babylon to the east.

Though the goods might originate half a world away, the caravans that transported them here to Jerusalem were local. Whether the caravans were stopping in Jerusalem or were just passing through, all of them stopped at the caravansary north of the city. It was there I went to find some answers.

The caravansary was a small walled city where travellers and caravans stopped to rest, feed and water their animals and themselves. At the caravansary I spoke with a man named Eziekial, who was the proprietor. I asked him if he remembered twelve men leaving Jerusalem over a week ago heading north to Galilee. He said he did not, so I asked if he recalled twelve men coming to Jerusalem from the north. Again he said he did not, but if I required information I might wish to speak to a Nabatean who is known to lead a caravan between Petra and Caesarea, and who was at this very moment entering the walls of the caravansary.

The Nabatean, whose name was Daretas, entered the caravansary leading a caravan of nine camels and riders. Camels were the ideal form of transportation in the desert. Each beast could carry half its weight and travel two weeks without water. They could close their wide nostrils during a sandstorm, and their large feet kept them surefooted in the shifting sands. The camels did have shortcomings; they were indiscriminate where and when they spat, and they smelled bad. Daretas was not unlike the camels in his caravan. He was a strong and tough old Arab who could go long distances in the desert, and like his camels he spat regularly and smelled bad. I did not believe he would willingly wish to supply me with information.

I found him amongst his camels. Like any good caravan leader he was seeing to the beasts on which he depended. I approached him and he eyed me suspiciously.

"You are Daretas the Nabatean?" I asked authoritatively.

"Who wants to know?" he replied tersely, and spat upon the ground. It was dark, and he obviously did not know who I was.

"I am Tribune Claudius Maximus." He stared at me as if he were expecting more. "I have reason to suspect you are transporting contraband." He continued to stare expectantly. "I am going to have my men go through your wares piece by piece until we find what I want…I mean, until we find the contraband."

The Nabatean's face finally dropped when the realization of his situation dawned on him, and his entire attitude changed to one more cooperative.

"Tribune," he said grinning almost evilly. "Tribune, how can I assist you? I have no contraband. Everything I carry is legal."

"I am certain if I search your packs I will find something of interest," I said slyly.

"Tribune, Tribune, that is not necessary. If you only tell me what you desire…I mean tell me what you think I have."

"I have it on good authority that you met up with ten or twelve Jews on the trail north of Jerusalem."

Daretas thought frantically trying to recall the incident.

"No," he said vaguely.

"No!" I repeated angrily. "I know you met them."

His eyes shifted like a cornered animal. "Yes!" he exclaimed as he squinted and nodded.

"But they were just travelling north. I had no contact with them."

"But I know you spoke with them!" I insisted.

"Yes," he replied hesitantly. "Yes, I did speak with them, but only in passing."

I glared at him doubtfully.

"I asked them to wither they travelled, and if they wished to join up with us."

"There was more," I said with certainty.

"No," he protested. "Yes. I asked them if they had anything to trade, but they did not."

"They gave you nothing?" I queried.

"Nothing, I swear. They seemed to be in a hurry. They travelled with haste, not stopping even to reply."

"Did they say where they hastened?"

"No. They were very unfriendly and rude; but then, they were Jews."

The last part, I am certain, he added to get into my good graces.

"These Jews," I said now that he was in the right frame of mind, "did you recall how many there were?"

"Ten, perhaps twelve."

"Did one seem to be wounded, or sick in any way?"

"No, they all looked young and healthy. As I told you, they were travelling quickly."

"Were they carrying a large bundle between them? Perhaps something wrapped up, about the size of a man."

"No," he replied. "A few carry bundles, but they were all small ones, perhaps small bundles of food and water for the journey, nothing more."

I turned and walked away.

"Tribune!" the Nabatean called out after me. "What about the contraband you wished for? Is there nothing you desire?"

"I have what I wanted," I said back to him.

I left Daretas and the caravansary and headed back for Jerusalem. If I were to find the disciples of Jesus I was certain Blind Man would know something by this time. I entered Jerusalem and I started for the Lower City. Lower City was in the southeast section of Jerusalem and was separated from Upper City by a high wall to keep the poor Jews from encroaching upon the rich Jews.

It was quite late and the streets were empty as I walked them, but I soon got that familiar feeling that I was being followed. Blind Man again. When will he ever learn? I decided to teach him a lesson he'd not soon forget. I turned a corner, ducked into a dark doorway and waited for him to come by. I heard his footsteps, and just as he approached I jumped out in front of him and yelled, hoping it would scare him enough to soil his garments. As I yelled, I heard a rush of air, and felt a sensation across my right forearm that was at first cold, then seemed to burn with the intensity of fire. With my left hand I grabbed my forearm and it felt wet. I was cut. I peered into the darkness to the figure who stood before me. It was not Blind Man. It was Marius, and by the moonlight I could see the glint of steel he held in his right hand. I instinctively reached inside my tunic for my dagger. It was not there. Marius took a step towards me. I took a step back. With a dagger I might have a chance against him. Without one, the odds were good of ending up on a cold slab with a coin on my mouth.

Marius took another step forward, and instead of stepping back, I moved in on Marius and kicked him between the legs as hard as I could. That kick would have crippled any normal man, but Marius was tough, and only crumpled slightly. Thinking quickly, I did the only thing I could. I turned and ran. Behind me I heard the man emit an angry grunt and in an instant was after me. I ran blindly, darting this way and that, choosing whatever opening was available. I stumbled and fell, rose up again and threw myself over a low wall and into a courtyard. Winded and tired I lay there by the wall waiting. I tried to slow my breath so Marius would not hear me. I do not know how long I lay there, my tongue parched, my heart beating as if in my head. Slowly I rose up to peer over the wall. Marius stood just opposite me on the other side of it. With a vile curse he lunged at me with his knife. I backed away and his lunge sent him over the wall and he fell to the ground. I dashed across the courtyard as he cried out my name. Fearing I was hopelessly lost, I desperately turned one corner after another until I found myself in a blind alleyway. With no other way out, I wheeled to retrace my steps, but by the dim moonlight I saw Marius standing in the mouth of the alley barring my way.

"This is the end for you, Maximus," he growled through clenched teeth. He began to move towards me. "I am going to cut out your heart!"

I backed away slowly and my foot brushed up against something. It was a ladder leaning against the building. In an instant I scrambled up the ladder, and just as quickly Marius was racing after me. I felt the blade of his knife slice my sandal. This only spurred me on all the quicker and I soon found myself on the roof of a two-storeyed building. I raced across the roof and was faced with the fact that I was trapped up here. Jumping to the ground held little hope. In the dark I could break a leg or my neck, and I did not believe Marius would hesitate to jump down after me. Another rooftop lay across the way, but I judged the distance and realized I was not up to the leap.

Marius was soon on the rooftop and I turned to face him. He moved towards me slowly. I could see that evil grin creep across his face as he held the dagger menacingly, moving it back and forth in front of him.

"Better for you had you never left Rome," Marius uttered.

Marius and I began to move around in a circle, he looking for an opening to slash or thrust, me trying to avoid either. We moved together, as in some primitive dance, and if either of us made a sound, I did not hear it. Marius feinted and lunged. I barely avoided it.

"Is this how Flavius got his, Centurion?" I put to him. "A stab in the dark?"

"Flavius was a young fool. He should never have talked to you. You are as much to blame for his death."

"I will wager that soldier you're reputed to have killed was struck down from behind," I chided him. "Why do you not just come for me, Centurion? I am not even armed."

"You are going to get yours slow, Maximus," he uttered. "I am going to cut you into little pieces. First I think I'll cut off your ears, then your nose. I am going to slice off your lips and hack off your fingers one at a time."

Marius made a few more lunges at me and cut me twice. I moved towards the edge of the rooftop. I could not evade his blade much longer. He was in better physical condition than I, and he held the dagger. He would wear me down and eventually his blade would find its mark. In order to survive this I would have to end it soon.

"I cannot imagine why Flavius would have felt any loyalty to a *saltatrix tonsa* like you; unless the two of you were very close" I taunted him. Intense anger flashed into his eyes. I had him. "From the moment I met you, Centurion, I knew you were the *irrumator* for the group; you have the knees for it." His body began to tremble with rage. I stood near the edge of the roof. "I do not blame you for what you are. It must be difficult to pleasure a woman with a *pipinna*."

Marius screamed with the intensity of an enraged bull, his eyes bulging, his face contorted. He lunged at me in uncontrollable anger. I was able to grab him in an armlock. Marius screamed like a wounded ox. He was strong. I held onto his arm and he spun me about as if I were an infant, and I thought he might throw me over the roof's edge. I held on tightly and bore down on his arm twisting it with all my might. Marius cried out in pain and dropped the dagger. I made the mistake of releasing my grip upon his arm and Marius used that to his advantage. Before I knew it, his hands were at my throat in an iron grip. I clutched at his hands but could not break his hold upon my throat. I dug my thumb into his left eye as if to pluck it out. Marius tightened his hold upon my throat and I stabbed my thumb in deeper. I could feel myself slipping away as everything began to grow dim. I feared I might lose this one. Surprisingly, it was Marius who gave in. The sound he emitted was a combination of a grunt and a scream, and he released his grip. I fell to my knees and attempted to regain my breath. Near the roof's edge I saw the dagger Marius had dropped. He must have seen it the same time, and we both dove for the blade simultaneously. I reached it first and rolled over to meet my adversary's attack. He fell on top of me as I brought up the dagger, but the force of his lunge pitched us off the roof. I recall seeing and endless starlit sky, then rows of rooftops. It was a strange sensation. For an instant it actually felt as if we were floating in air and we would drift down slowly and safely to the ground below. This idea was dashed from my mind as the ground came up to meet us and we landed rather violently, me on top of Marius. I felt the air forced out of my body and wondered if I were dead. An indescribable, searing agony raced through my body and told me I was not. I rolled off of Marius and lay staring up at the night sky. I rose up with a groan and looked at the body next to me. Marius lay upon his back, the blade of the dagger had sunk deep into his chest.

Life had not yet fled his body. He seemed too tough to die. I knelt next to Marius and called him by name. His laboured breathing was growing sporadic, and he began to cough up blood. I knew he did not have much longer.

"Marius, did you kill Flavius? Why did you kill him? Was it Caiaphas you met at the theatre?" I asked desperately. "Did he give you more money? Was it for killing Flavius? Or was it to kill me?"

Gurgling wet sounds came out of his mouth from deep down in his throat.

"What happened at the tomb that morning?" I persisted. "Do you know the whereabouts of Lucius Drusus? Where are the disciples hiding?"

Marius let out one last long breath, and I knew that as that breath left his body, so did his damned soul.

I left Marius where he lay, in the dirt, covered in blood, with his own dagger stuck in his chest. As for me, it was a long walk back to my quarters. I left a trail of blood from the cuts I received. When I finally reached my rooms I thought I might pass out. Fortunately for me Ruth was there to clean me up and bandage my wounds. Sometimes I wondered why she did it. Neither of us spoke much and I eyed her suspiciously recalling Mary Magdalene's words that they were acquainted, and I wondered just how much.

"The cut is deep," Ruth commented. "Keep the wrapping clean and dry."

"It would not have been this bad if I had my dagger with me. I cannot seem to find it," I said and asked her: "Have you seen it?"

"Is it so important to you?" she asked, not bothering to meet my eyes.

"It was a gift from my father," I stated, while sensing some evasion on her part. "The dagger has...sentimental value. Have you seen it?"

Ruth stopped what she was doing and walked into the adjoining room. Seconds later she returned with my dagger in its scabbard. Ruth offered it to me and I took it. I gave her a questioning look and she said: "I took it and hid it amongst my things."

"In Jupiter's name, why?" I asked incredulously.

"I loathe that thing. I could not bear if you were to take someone's life with it."

"Thanks to your touching sentiment, the reverse almost came true."

We were both overcome by another bout of silence. It seemed so loud I thought I would go mad. I needed to end it.

"So, you told Mary Magdalene about me," I blurted out.

Ruth paused, and remained perfectly still, as in a wall painting. "You spoke with her?" she asked hesitantly.

"Yes."

"Did you learn what you wished to know?"

"Not as much as I hoped. I still do not know where to find the body of Jesus. Perhaps Magdalene knows, but she is not saying."

"She does not know!" Ruth exclaimed. She seemed more surprised by her exclamation than I.

"How do you know she does not?" I asked her, not hiding my suspicion.

"I simply know," she answered. "She is a good woman. I trust her."

"Do you know what she is?" I said accusingly. "Do you know the things she's done?"

"I know what she has done!" Ruth came back with anger. "I also know that part of her life is over, and she has a new life now."

"Have you ever seen a zebra?" I put to her, my own anger beginning to rise. "They live in Africa and look like a horse but they are striped black and white, and try as they may a zebra can never be a horse. It cannot change its stripes."

"But a person can change, Claudius, if she is willing. No matter what she may have done in the past, she can start life over and begin a new life in Jesus."

"Where did you hear that from? Magdalene?" I said. "Do not allow that woman to fill your pretty head with ideas of a miracle man that can turn water into wine, and rise from the dead. Magdalene is a whore, pure and simple. She could no more change what she is than you could."

For a brief instant Ruth glared at me with sheer loathing. It was a look I had never witnessed on her before, and not imagined her capable of baring. But then it was gone and I saw her face, her entire body collapsed in pain and hurt. A terrible sob escaped her. She pressed the back of her hand to her mouth and turned away from me. Her body convulsed in heaping sobs. For some reason, it pained me to see her that way. I suspected it was something I said that hurt her.

Against my better judgement I said: "I am sorry."

Ruth continued to cry, then she turned and ran into my arms. I held her.

"Please, Claudius, never say that to me again," she said through her tears.

I was not certain to what she referred, but I said I would not.

"And you will cease looking for the body of Jesus and his disciples," she added.

"You know I cannot do that."

"But why must you?"

I felt the hint of female manipulation and I was repulsed by it.

"Do not push me woman!" I shouted, grabbing her two shoulders and holding her at arms length. "I have had an awful day. I killed a man tonight. He was a fellow Roman soldier. He may not have been a good one, but he was my own kind. Do you believe I would think twice about breaking *your* neck?!"

A calm sadness came over her. Now, that was a look I had seen on her before.

Ruth unconsciously raised her hand to the side of her head and touched it gingerly as if it were tender. "I fully know what you are capable of doing, Claudius Maximus," she said with hidden resentment. "The strange part is; I love you regardless."

And as if she said she was going to the market for fruit, Ruth walked out.

CHAPTER XVIII

▼

Ruth did not come home that night nor the next morning. I waited until almost midday.

I decided to go out and my first stop was at the praetorium. I found Titus and Scarus. They did not want to speak with me, but I did not care. The day was hot, and I was in no mood for their reticence. This had gone on long enough. I had been through too much to hold back now. If they did not want to talk to me, then I would talk to them.

"The two of you are going to tell me what happened that morning at the tomb," I spoke to them forcefully. "Flavius already told me what happened, and I need the two of you to confirm it."

"Flavius told you and now he is dead," Titus said, not concealing his contempt.

"If we tell you, we are as good as dead ourselves," Scarus added.

"Marius killed Flavius, didn't he?" I said and spoke as if I were certain.

They exchanged uneasy glances and it was Scarus who spoke reluctantly: "We swore an oath not to tell anyone. If we tell you, then Marius would certainly kill us." It was evident they feared Marius.

"That is not going to happen," I told them. "Right now Marius is paying the ferryman for a ride across the River Styx."

"Marius is dead!" Titus responded with unbelief.

"Do you know how it happened?" Scarus asked me.

"That is of no consequence," I said. "Did either of you speak with Marius lately?"

"I did," Scarus spoke up.

"Did Marius make reference to meeting anyone at the theatre the other day?"

Scarus's face went slack as he stopped to think. It was like watching a squad of raw recruits trying to get an old siege machine up and running. Finally his deep voice spoke slowly and methodically. "Marius did say something about meeting someone…I think…he said…he was going to see…the high priest!"

I smiled and slapped his broad shoulder. Scarus smiled back showing a few missing teeth.

I could tell that Titus and Scarus had now changed their attitude towards me. The death of Marius had left a gap in their lives they needed filled—someone who would lead them and who could do their thinking for them. Both were quick and eager to have me fill the position, and I decided to take advantage of the situation.

"Men," I said, mustering all the camaraderie I could display without making myself ill, "what is important now, is that you tell me exactly what occurred that morning at the tomb."

Anxious to please, both told their account, which corroborated Flavius's story.

I told them they were fine soldiers and that I may be in need of their services very soon, so they should stand ready for when I called.

I left the praetorium and decided to pay an unexpected call on Joseph Caiaphas.

The high priest's palace was situated in the southwestern corner of Jerusalem in a section referred to as the Essene Quarter. The palace was surrounded by high walls with locked and guarded gates. At the main gate I informed a servant that I wished to see the high priest on official business. Of course the reply came back that the high priest could not see me. I, in turn, sent back a message that if the high priest did not see me here and now, I would be back with a squad of armed soldiers. A short time later, the servant returned and showed me into a spacious courtyard with a pool in the centre. There were, of course, no statues around the pool—Hebrew religion prohibited graven images—but the courtyard was decorated with well-trimmed bushes and ornamental trees. Despite the shade from the trees, the heat of the day was uncomfortable, and I scooped out handfuls of water from the pool onto my face and wrists. After a time, Caiaphas met with me by the pool. He did not seem pleased to see me.

Caiaphas studied my bandages and cuts, then remarked: "Ah, Tribune, your appearance is a constant surprise to me, as is your presence here.

"I am seriously considering making a formal protest to the Praetor and the Prefect regarding your persistent harassment," the high priest stated. His manner of dress appeared less formal than when I met him in the Royal Portico. His demeanour was more hostile. "It was one thing to question me at the Temple, but to threaten your way into my home is quite another. I can say without prejudice that you have overstepped your bounds and abused your authority. Emperor Tiberias will certainly be distressed to learn of your reprehensible behaviour."

"Threats only work if a man believes the person threatening him will actually go through with them," I said unbothered. "And I do not believe you will."

"Oh. Why is that?"

"Because then you will have to answer some embarrassing questions from someone with more authority than I."

"And what might those be?"

"Out of the four guards who guarded Jesus's tomb, two are dead. One of them, a young soldier named Flavius told me the truth about what actually occurred. He told me you paid all of them to not speak of it, and if anyone were to ask they were to tell a falsehood about Jesus's followers stealing the body in the night."

"Yes, yes, yes," Caiaphas said impatiently. "We went through all this before."

"Yes, unfortunately Flavius is now dead; this I believe you know. But what you may not know is that the leader of the four, Marius by name, is now also dead."

"How would I know about the death of this man Flavius?" Caiaphas asked.

"Marius told you when you met him at the theatre," I stated.

"I did not speak with the centurion Marius at the theatre."

"Do you ever grow weary of lying?" I uttered.

"Please dispense with the insults, Tribune, and stick to the facts of the matter. If I say I did not speak with Marius, then you may believe that I did not."

"I saw the two of you together at the theatre," I said with conviction. "You and Marius spoke briefly, and you handed him something—most likely more money. You left the theatre separately. I followed you to the Temple and you went inside."

"You actually saw me?" Caiaphas said looking at me in such a way I now began to doubt my suspicions. "You saw my face?"

"No," I stated plainly. "Your face was hidden by a hood."

"Then may I suggest that you were mistaken, Tribune."

"I have it on good authority that Marius said he was going to meet with the high priest the other day. If Marius did not meet with you at the theatre, then who was it?"

"Am I interrupting something?"

Caiaphas and I turned our heads in the direction of the voice. Standing on the opposite side of the pool was an elderly man in his sixties, dressed in priestly robes. His hazel eyes went from me to Caiaphas then back to me again. He looked familiar but I could not recall where I had seen him before.

"No, Jabez, you are not interrupting," Caiaphas spoke, taking on a friendlier tone. "May I present Tribune Claudius Maximus. Tribune, this is my father-in-law, Jabez Annas."

Of course, I thought to myself, Annas was once high priest of the Temple, and though he no longer held that position, his influence and power in Jerusalem were known to me. He would have made a good Roman.

Annas walked around the pool to join us. He studied my appearance and said: "Why, young man, you do look as if you came upon some unpleasant difficulty."

As I watched him move, things became clearer and the realization thrust itself upon me.

"It was you I saw with Marius the other day at the theatre," I revealed to Annas.

Caiaphas said: "What?" But the older man only smiled at me.

"It was you," I persisted. "You met Marius, spoke with him, passed something to him and then you walked to the Temple."

"Tribune, what are you saying?" Caiaphas demanded of me, but I did not take my eyes from Annas.

Annas did not look guilty in any way, but simply stated: "Yes, you are quite correct."

"What are you saying?" Caiaphas asked his father-in-law.

Annas turned to the high priest and said: "Marius came to me and asked for money."

Caiaphas looked at me guiltily and then motioned to Annas to be silent.

The older man smiled without worry. "My dear Joseph, the Tribune has his suspicions, but he will not be able to prove anything. Even if I say here and now that I gave Marius money, I will not repeat it."

"Can you tell me why you gave him money?" I asked.

"Though I am under no obligation to do so, I will tell you," Annas said to me. "Marius told me he had killed his fellow-soldier, and to remain quiet about it, he required payment. He also said you were a threat that needed to be eliminated."

"So you paid him to kill me?" I accused him angrily.

Annas regarded me soberly. "I tell you truthfully, Tribune, that I did not pay, nor did I encourage Marius to harm you in any way. Any action Marius may take against you is entirely his own doing."

It was Caiaphas who spoke next. "The Tribune has informed me that Marius is dead."

Annas appeared surprised at this disclosure, and he regarded me suspiciously. "Yes, I see," he said slowly.

"Did Marius say why he killed Flavius?" I asked.

"I believe you already have your suspicions regarding that, Tribune, but I will not say."

"Why have you not told me all this before?" Caiaphas asked Annas.

"I would have eventually," Annas responded with a hint of condescension. "I know you have been very busy as of late, and I thought to relieve you of this one burden."

"The same way you did not tell me that you had Jesus taken to your house for questioning before he was brought here?" Caiaphas said accusatorially.

"Then how do you know?" Annas asked him.

"I, too, have my sources," Caiaphas said, revealing his resentment. "It would be well for you to remember that you are no longer the high priest of the Temple—I am!"

"And you, dear Joseph, would do well to remember that you would not be high priest if not for me! If you have any doubt of that, or have grown tired of your position, I have other sons that could well fill the position!"

The forceful way in which the older man spoke caused Caiaphas to look away and he said no more. It was becoming clear who actually held the power in this family. If Caiaphas was in any way corrupt or dishonest, he was a mere shadow compared to Annas.

Annas turned to me with a bit more civility than he showed his son-in-law. "As for you, Tribune, you can prove nothing. We, of course, will admit nothing. If you are looking for the body of the Nazarene, you best find it quickly. If you are searching for his disciples, my sources tell me they have fled to Galilee. Either way, I do not believe you pose any threat to us."

"It is not my duty to pose a threat," I remarked. "As for proof, I have two of the remaining Roman guards who will swear what occurred at the tomb, and that they reported it to Caiaphas, and that the high priest gave them money to lie about it. It will be the word of two Romans against the word of two Hebrews. I know which Pontius Pilate will believe. Good day, gentlemen."

CHAPTER XIX

▼

If there was one thing I could not stomach, it was hypocrisy. If a man plans to steal to fill his own purse, let him go into politics and be honest about it. But to hide behind religion, and masquerade as a godly man looking out for the welfare of the people, only to further his own ends, makes my innards churn. It only goes to prove the old saying is true; *pecuniae obedieunt omnia*—all things yield to money.

I left Annas and Caiaphas in each others company—they truly deserved one another—and I started off for home. I was in hopes that Ruth would return soon, so I could ask her to contact Mary Magdalene for me. It was important that I speak with the disciples. After all *parturient montes, nascetur ridiculus mus*—with all my efforts I had little to show for it.

Ruth was not home, and though I waited for some time she did not return. Waiting around did not sit well with me, so I left in hopes of finding her through word on the street. After a futile search and finding no one who knew her where-abouts, I decided to put Blind Man to work. I found him in his usual spot out-side the main gate on the western wall.

"So you finally show up," said Blind Man as he sat on his worn old mat with a wooden bowl in his hands. "I have been looking for you all morning."

"So what are you doing here?" I asked.

"A man must earn a living."

"I am looking for Ruth. Have you seen her?"

"No, I have not. But I do have important information," the beggar responded and he held up his bowl.

"Just the other day I gave you a denarius," I said, irritated.

"What I have to say is worth more than that."

From my purse I deposited one more silver denarius, and if Blind Man even looked dissatisfied, I planned on breaking his arm.

He took my offering, and for a brief instant he considered holding out for more, but my manner must have betrayed my thoughts, for when he studied my face he reconsidered his position.

"I trust this is all you have on your person," he commented with an even tone, "but what I have to tell you is so important I am certain you will wish to reward me further in the near future."

"If you do not tell me immediately what you have found, you will get your reward right here and now, and you will never live to see the near future."

Blind Man considered this briefly and said: "I have found the disciples and their hiding place."

"Where?" I said, calmly.

"It is worth much, is it not?"

"Where?" I repeated in a tone Blind Man knew well.

"They are hiding in a building in the Essene Quarter," he said racing to get the words out of his mouth. "There may be sentries watching from the main floor and I am certain the doors are barred."

"You will take me there now," I told him hastily, and then rethought the matter. "No, wait. First we will go to the praetorium and enlist the aid of some mindless muscle."

"I have an idea," Blind Man stated. "While you go to the praetorium, I will stay here and earn what I can until you return." Again he read my mood and reconsidered. "I will go with you now."

At the praetorium, I found Titus and Scarus. They were eager to follow me to hades itself with no questions asked. Neither of them even hesitated when I told them to bring along a small battering ram.

Blind Man led us to a large two-storey building in the Essene Quarter that, ironically enough, was not far from the grand house of Joseph Caiaphas. It was an inconspicuous dwelling with few windows. A wall encircled it with one gate out front and a small gate in back. Both gates were closed by a heavy wooden door that was securely barred. Somehow this building looked familiar. It took me a moment to realize that this was the same dwelling Mary Magdalene had stopped at before and almost entered the night I saw her on the street. Her strange behaviour that night of stopping at different doorways had bewildered me until now. That night, as she was prepared to enter this place—the hiding place of the disciples—she must have suspected she was being watched and had almost revealed the disciples' hiding place. Mary Magdalene then attempted to divert attention away from this house by going to different doors and repeating her actions. In this way she hoped it would not be clear what door she wished to enter.

I suspected the back gate would be easiest to breach, so we concentrated on that. I instructed Blind Man to position himself by the front gate, and if anyone were to come running out, he was to follow them.

After Scarus tested the rear gate, he nodded to Titus. The two used the battering ram, and after a few blows, the gate yielded. With some haste we made our way to the rear door of the building. Titus and Scarus repeated the procedure and we gained entry into the dwelling. At first, the building appeared deserted. There was no sign of any guards that Blind Man had spoke of, but I hoped we would find someone. I placed Titus at the rear door, and Scarus at the front door, while I searched the rooms on the main floor. The first room I entered was empty. From down the hall came strange sounds, as if someone moaning in pain. The door to the room was closed but not locked. I was not certain what I would find on the other side of the door. I wiped the sweat from my brow and licked my dry lips, then opened the door and entered. The room was small and the only furniture in it was a sleeping cot in the far corner. On the cot lay the figure of a large man with his back to me. It was clear the man was in extreme pain from the manner in which he was moaning and the way he held himself, with his knees drawn up and his hands clutching his belly. His tunic was bathed in sweat. I approached him and, laying a hand on his shoulder, I asked: "Are you ill or wounded? Can I aid you? What is wrong with you?"

The man turned to face me. Even with his features contorted in agony I recognized him, though I had not expected to see him here.

"Drusus!" I exclaimed. "What has happened to you? What are you doing here?"

He motioned to answer, but could not. Despite his pain he managed to say my name, then his eyes looked to the door, and I knew someone stood there. I whirled around with my dagger ready. As surprised as I was at finding Lucius Drusus here, I was shocked when I turned and faced:

"Ruth!" I exclaimed. We stared at one another for an instant, both of us struck dumb. Finally I found my voice. It spilled out with anger.

"What is the meaning of this? What are you doing here? What is this man doing here? What ails him? Speak woman!"

In her arms, she carried a familiar small bundle of linen and alabastrons of medicinal oils. She walked past me to kneel by the bedside of Drusus.

"You should not have come here," Ruth said to me as she attended the centurion. "I wish you would leave this place, Claudius."

Though her voice was pleading, my heart was hardened by feelings of betrayal.

"I have come here for answers," I stated, "and I am not leaving until I get them. What are you doing here?"

"I am trying to comfort this man by relieving his pain until he heals," Ruth said.

"Heals from what?" I asked. "Has he been wounded?"

As an answer she lifted his tunic and removed the wrappings underneath.

"By Jupiter!" I cried. "What have they done to him? Have they tortured him?"

Drusus's moans and cries increased and he began to thrash about.

"Hold him still while I change his dressing," Ruth instructed me with such authority I did not consider refusing. I knelt next to her and gripped the centurion's arms and bore down on him.

As Ruth administered to Drusus, she explained. "Lucius came here to speak with the disciples."

"So Drusus is in league with them!" I said. "They needed Drusus's help to save their friend from death on the cross."

Ruth shook her head and appeared perturbed. "Do not be ridiculous, Claudius. Drusus never helped them in any way."

"Then why is he here?"

"Lucius has renounced his old life and is here to become a follower of Jesus the Christ."

"I do not believe it," I said.

Ruth looked me in the eye and asked: "Why would I lie to you?"

I could not think of a reason, and she continued.

"Lucius was told that if he cared to become a true disciple of the Christ Jesus, he would have to be circumcised."

"What?!"

"It is an ancient rite of my people that all males are to be circumcised. Circumcision is when—"

"I know what circumcision is," I stated. "And I know that it is extremely painful when performed upon a grown man."

"Precisely," Ruth said. "As for why I am here…"

"You are here because Mary Magdalene has convinced you to become a disciple also. I knew that woman was trouble."

"You are wrong, Claudius. You do not know her."

"And you do?"

"When Mary told me her story, it was as if she were telling my story, as if she were speaking of me. Never before had I heard things more clearly. She put into words feelings I did not even know I had. All my deep thoughts, fears and longing. She knows me and I know her. Mary showed me that my life can be something other than what it is. It can be honest and righteous and true. I need not live in fear and hate and loathing; loathing of myself and…others."

"You believe you can start your life over?" I sneered.

"Is that so wrong?" she asked me.

"Nothing good came come of this," I told her. "These people will ruin you. Their time has passed. Their leader is dead! They are trouble, and you should stay clear of them."

"You are wrong, Claudius," she said. "If you would only speak with the disciples."

"What do you think…" I stopped. Knowing Ruth as I did, I decided to change my tactics.

"Perhaps you are right," I said, easing my tone. "If only I had an opportunity to speak with them, I could understand what you mean."

"Why, they are right here in the upper room…" Ruth stopped and studied my face. She realized how she had betrayed herself. "Oh, Claudius, please don't go up there!"

I rose and left the room with the sound of Ruth calling me back. I shouted for Titus and Scarus. They came and followed me up a flight of stairs that led to the second floor. At the top of stairs was a door. I tried to open the door but it was heavily barred. I motioned to my companions, and, with the aid of their battering ram, they forced the door.

"Stay out here," I instructed them, and I entered the room.

The upper room was large and spacious, furnished with tables and chairs and sleeping cots. There was only one door and one small window. Inside were huddled eleven men. By their dress and appearance I could see they were all Hebrews. One of them I recognized as the young man who sat in my quarters and introduced himself to me as John. They all stood back from the door and faced me with suspicion and a trace of fear.

"I am Tribune Claudius Maximus," I announced. "I am here under orders of the Emperor, and I am looking for the disciples of a Galilean named Jesus." The men stared at me silently, not knowing what to expect. "Which of you claims to be the leader?"

There were uneasy glances between them. Finally, one man stepped forward. He was tall, dark and confident.

"What is your name?" I asked him.

"My name is Peter," he said, and I remembered John mentioning that name.

"I would speak with you, Peter," I informed him, and I motioned to a far corner of the room.

From four paces apart we watched one another closely as we walked away from the rest to talk in private. Peter regarded me with heavy brows drawn down on dark eyes held in a squint as the result of working under the sun his entire life. His limbs were lean with some muscle from steady work.

"You know who I am?" I asked and he nodded. "You know why I am here?" He nodded again. "I am attempting to locate the body of Jesus of Nazareth."

"Why?" Peter asked.

"Never mind why," I spoke with some irritation and resentment. "If you know where the body is, you best tell me, here and now."

"I do not know where the body is," Peter told me sincerely.

"Do you know who took it?"

Peter scrutinized me closely. He obviously had been told about me by John, and Mary Magdalene, and possibly even Ruth. Now he was trying to decide for himself what sort of man stood before him.

"Before I can answer your question, I feel I must tell you a story," he stated.

I did not think this an unreasonable request, so I nodded. I stood with my legs spread wide and my arms crossed on my chest.

"I am originally from Bethsaida, on the Sea of Galilee's north shore," Peter began. "My name was Simon. Along with Philip and my brother Andrew"—here he motioned to two men standing off with the others—"we were fishermen in Capernaum. One day, about three years ago, Andrew and Philip brought a man to the boats by the shore. He said his name was Jesus, and he was like no man I had ever met. He gave me a new name, Peter, which means 'rock'. I left the fishing boats and nets behind, never to return to that manner of life again. We all left our former lives." Here again he indicated the others in the room and named them. "Beside Andrew and Philip, there is John, whom I believe you met, his brother James, Bartholomew, Matthew, Thomas, James son of Alphaeus, Simon, and Judas."

"Judas Iscariot?" I asked.

"No," Peter replied. "This is Judas, son of James. We sometimes call him Thaddaeus. The other Judas is no longer with us, but I will get to him.

"Jesus became our *rabboni*—our master, our teacher—and we were his disciples, his students. As is the custom with our people, we disciples lived and travelled with our *rabboni*. We watched everything he did and listened to all he said.

We tried to emulate him in every way. He would teach to people during the day, and at night he would instruct us privately. Jesus would ask us questions regarding what we observed that day, and we would attempt to explain and interpret these events. As we travelled from town to town, we watched how he ministered to people, teaching them, helping them grow closer to God. There was something else."

He hesitated, but I suspected what was next.

"He performed miracles. You may find this difficult to believe, but Jesus cured people of illnesses, fed thousands with a meagre portion, healed lepers, restored sight to the blind, made the cripple walk, walked on water, and more than once he raised the dead."

"And Jesus was able to perform these miracles because he believed he was the Son of God?" I asked sceptically.

"It was not because he believed it, or because we believed it; it was because Jesus was truly the Son of God."

I regarded Peter doubtfully.

"Tribune," he began in earnest, "how may I make you understand in one hour, or one day what has taken my brothers and myself years of intense teaching, and personal witness to come to believe? I cannot. I can only tell you what I know. And this I know; Jesus is the Messiah, the Christ who came into this world as a man to live and experience human existence. He was one of us, part of us. He spoke of love, brotherhood, forgiveness, and God's kingdom. And how was he rewarded for this? He was nailed to a cross to suffer and die."

"He was a threat to the Empire," I uttered weakly, but even I did not believe it.

Peter grinned as if he knew I did not believe it, and said: "You could not have stopped it if you wanted to. You see, he was our example. This is what we must go through if necessary to spread God's word. He was saying to us, 'If I can do it, you can do it.'"

"But for what purpose?" I asked, and realized it was becoming my favourite question.

"For the same purpose we do anything," Peter said. "For the greater glory of God."

"Your God," I responded.

He shook his head and said: "The God of all men, all creation. The one true God."

Peter spoke for some time. He never grew tired of talking, and I never grew tired of listening to him. Occasionally I would utter a question or interjection, but he continued to speak of Jesus. He spoke of parables, lepers, and storms that were quelled with a gesture, of desert sojourns, and temptations, of a sermon on a mountain, and seeing Moses and Elias. He spoke of a baptism and a beheading."

"Exactly who was John the Baptist?" I asked, recalling Salome's tale.

"John the Baptist was a desert prophet who foretold the coming of our Lord, Jesus. He would baptize people in the River Jordan. One day our Lord came to the river to be baptized, but John recognized Jesus and wished to be baptized by him instead. It was soon after that we became the disciples of Jesus. John continued to preach of God's kingdom that would come. Then one day he was arrested and taken to the tetrarch, Herod Antipas. John offended Herod and his wife and her daughter, by stating that their marriage was not in keeping with God's law. Herod had John the Baptist put up in the dungeon for a time before he was beheaded. After we heard what had happened, we took John's body and laid it in a tomb. Jesus was much distressed at the death of John the Baptist."

I said: "Tell me what happened when Jesus came to Jerusalem the last time."

Peter smiled at the memory, but there was sadness in his smile. "He entered Jerusalem riding a donkey's colt, as was foretold in ancient prophecy. The people laid palm branches before him, and praised him. Later, in the Temple, our Lord displayed his distress at seeing the money changers conducting business there. If you have ever been to the Temple, Tribune, you yourself must have seen the money changers and animal sellers there. Jesus drove them out. Some say these people provide a necessary service, but it was the view of our Lord that the Temple was a holy place, not a place of business."

"Did he speak of destroying the Temple?" I asked recalling Caiaphas's words.

Peter appeared uncomfortable, but nodded. "Yes, Jesus did remark that the Temple would be destroyed, but we did not always understand the things he said. I do not believe he meant he personally would destroy the Temple—for it still stands."

"Then what did he mean?" I asked.

Peter thought a moment, then responded: "Perhaps he meant that he was the Temple. That the Temple in Jerusalem is, after all, just a building of stone, and cannot compare with the Son of God. And that we should worship him, and that we can worship him in our hearts. When Jesus said 'destroy the Temple' I believe he was referring to his own death."

"And when he said 'rebuild it in three days'," I queried, "he was referring to his resurrection?"

Peter would not say, but uttered: "Whatever he meant, he did not ingratiate himself with the Pharisees. Several times they came and tried to ensnare our Lord with questions regarding our law, and attempting to unveil him as an enemy of the Romans. Every time Jesus escaped their entrapments.

"Now came the time for the Passover *Seder*, or supper. It is a special feast in which we, as a people, recall our delivery out of bondage from the Egyptians. The *Seder* we shared with Jesus was in this very room.

"Jesus first took a towel, girded himself, filled a foot basin with water and began to wash our feet. We were, of course, uncomfortable to see him in this role—this was a servant's duty. We should have been washing *his* feet. When we mentioned this to him, Jesus told us that we may not know now why he does this thing, but we would know later. You see, Tribune, he was setting us an example. We must serve others to serve God.

"Later, at the Seder he announced that the food we ate was his body, and the wine we drank was his blood."

"His blood," I repeated confused by it all. Then I recalled something and said to Peter: "The centurion, Drusus, who witnessed the crucifixion, told me that when Jesus was pierced by a spear his blood ran out with water."

Peter nodded at this and remarked: "The water of baptism and the blood of Christ will save us."

"Save us from what?"

"From the damnation caused by own sinful lives."

I did not pretend to understand, and Peter did not explain.

"It was soon after this that Jesus denounced Judas," said Peter.

"Judas Iscariot," I uttered. "Tell me of him."

Peter began to speak of Iscariot with neither shame nor ridicule. "Judas was one of us. He was our brother. And like any of us, he was not perfect. Why he betrayed our Lord, I believe none of us will ever know."

"Was it the money?" I asked.

"If it were," Peter replied in the same manner he began, "does that make him any less human, any less of a lost soul? Does it matter all that much?"

"It matters to me," I stated. "I must know to make my report complete. Did any of you resent Iscariot at all for anything?"

"At times there was loose talk regarding Judas not being totally honest, but our Lord accepted him, and so did we."

"So you do not believe any of your brethren killed him?"

Peter looked neither shocked nor dismayed, but simply said: "None of us killed him, nor did any of us save him."

"You sound regretful," I observed.

"No one wanted, or believed it would end like this. No one except…" Peter let his statement trail off. I prompted him, and he said: "Except Jesus himself."

"Do you mean to say he wanted to die on the cross?"

Peter looked half bewildered. "It is not simple to explain, but he knew it would happen. He told us so. But even then, I do not think any of us believed it would happen this way."

"So he had oracle powers," I concluded. "Jesus could tell the future."

"Not the way you would believe," Peter remarked. "But he did know things. He knew Judas would betray him. He knew where we would find the colt for him to ride on into Jerusalem. He told us how we would find this room for the *Seder*, and he knew I would deny him."

"What do you mean, deny him?"

"On the night of the *Seder*, he spoke of leaving us, of going away. When Thomas said that none of us may know the way, Jesus replied, 'I am the way, the truth, and the light. No one may come to the Father, but through me."

"What did he mean by that?" I asked Peter.

"He often spoke that way," Peter replied. "We did not always know what he meant. But we professed our love and devotion. Then he said something to me that was insulting. Jesus told me I would deny knowing him three times. I, in turn, told him that would never happen."

"And?"

"I am embarrassed to admit I did exactly what Jesus said I would do. But I am getting ahead of the story. After the *Seder*, Jesus had the eleven of us follow him—Judas having left the room when Jesus denounced him as his betrayer. Jesus led us out of Jerusalem by the south gate, and circled the south wall of the city, through the Kidron Valley, up the Mount of Olives east of the city to a garden called Gethsemane. It is a beautiful spot, even at night. It is a very peaceful place, and Jesus wanted to pray. He had gone there often in the past when he wished to pray and think. He told us to wait, while he went off by himself. That was also something he did occasionally. Unfortunately it was late. We were tired, and subsequently we fell asleep. Jesus came back and found us sleeping, and rebuked us for it. We fell asleep a second time, and when we finally came awake, Jesus was there, and he knew who and what was coming even before we saw the torches bouncing up the hillside, or heard the clanging of armour and weapons. His betrayer had come leading a mob of soldiers, and slaves and priests."

"How did Iscariot know Jesus would be in the garden?" I asked.

"As I said before, Jesus had previously visited the spot many times, with and without us. Judas might have overheard the master's intention of going back there, or he may simply have guessed Jesus would be there."

"So, they came to arrest him," I stated, prompting Peter to continue.

"Yes," Peter said thoughtfully. "Judas had come to deliver Jesus to his enemies."

"He put up no resistance, but one of you did."

"Yes," said Peter, "I did. I could not stand to see them take him. I drew one of the soldiers' swords and struck a servant of Caiaphas who was moving to lay hands upon the master."

"Did you know the servant's name?" I asked.

"His name, I believe, is Malchus."

"Do you know where I can find him?" I asked. Peter said he did not. Then I asked: "Is it true what happened?"

"Is what true?"

"That you wounded the man with the sword." That was all I would say. I wanted Peter to finish, and he did.

"I struck Malchus here," Peter told me, and he indicated the left ear. "But our Lord stepped forward and put an end to the violence."

"Then what did Jesus do?" I asked.

"He approached the servant, Malchus, and healed his wound."

"What happened then?"

"They took away our Lord to the house of Annas, the former high priest. Out of fear, we had fled, but I followed them from afar. I waited outside the house of Annas, and when they came out again they took Jesus to the house of Caiaphas. I waited in the court with his servants by the fire. While I waited, three different people accused me of knowing Jesus and being one of his followers. Out of fear I denied knowing him. I was afraid they might arrest me also. When I realized I had denied Jesus, as he said I would, I fled the scene and wept for my weak will and character."

I then questioned Peter regarding the crucifixion. What he told me very closely resembled what I already knew. He had also been there at the cave when they prepared Jesus's body for burial, and sealed him up inside the tomb.

"And you never returned to the tomb?" I asked.

"After his burial, all of us you see here were locked up in this room behind a barred door from the evening of the crucifixion, all of the next day, and the morning of the third day."

"What happened the morning of the third day?" I asked.

"Mary Magdalene came pounding on our door that morning. We let her in and she was very excited, almost frantic. She was wringing her hands and pacing about. She told us that she had just come from the tomb of our Lord, and his body was gone. We all agreed, out of safety sake, that only John and I would accompany her to the tomb to see for ourselves."

"You did not believe her?" I asked him.

"We had to see for ourselves," Peter said. "We had been through much. We were frightened and distraught. Being locked up in this room for so long we began to bicker amongst ourselves. When we arrived at the tomb, it was as Mary had told us—the tomb was empty. At first I thought the Sanhedrin had taken the body, then I thought perhaps it was taken by Romans."

"Why would the Sanhedrin or the Romans take the body?" I asked.

"They wanted to be rid of Jesus, didn't they?" Peter remarked with some resentment. "Perhaps they wished to eradicate all evidence that he ever existed. Did you ever stop to consider that?"

I thought on this a moment and said with half a grin: "They believe you took the body, and you believe they took the body."

"That was only my first impression," Peter spoke. "Everything changed that night in this very room."

"What happened?"

"John and I returned here after we visited the tomb," Peter began. "A short time later Mary came again, pounding on the door, demanding entry. We let her in and she appeared very nervous and agitated. She was even more excited than before. Her eyes looked wild and alive. On her face there was an ever-present grin that I can only describe as half-joyful half-fearful. She appeared very nervous and agitated. Mary claimed that after we left her she saw Jesus—alive! She had spoken with him! We did not know what to believe. We thought Mary had imagined it all, for we did not believe she would deliberately lie to us. Mary said that Jesus had told her that we were to go to Galilee. After we discussed the matter amongst ourselves, we thought it best to send Mary away, and we would remain here. I remember Thomas was very opposed to believing Mary's account. 'Unless I see in his hands the prints of the nails, and put my finger there,' Thomas had said, indicating the side where Jesus was pierced by a spear, 'I will not believe.' We did not wish to risk going out into the streets where we might be seen and arrested. Later that evening, as we sat here discussing what we should do next, he appeared."

"Who appeared?"

"Our Lord Jesus appeared in this very room!" Peter stated.

I looked at him doubtfully and asked: "How is that possible? Was the door not barred? Is there a secret passage into this room?"

"The door was barred as when you broke in, Tribune," Peter said. "There is no secret way into this room, you may look for yourself."

"Are you telling me it was his ghost, his spirit?" I proposed.

Peter shook his head, and there was a slight smile on his lips. He said: "It was not his spirit we saw, Tribune; it was Jesus in the flesh. And yet he was not exactly the same as when we had known him."

I was not certain I understood what Peter was trying to say. I was not certain Peter himself understood what he was trying to say.

"What did Jesus do?" I asked Peter. "What did he say?"

Peter spoke, and there was suppressed excitement in his voice. In his face appeared both a calmness and strength of spirit I had seen only in one other person. "'Peace be with you,' Jesus greeted us. We were all shocked to see him. He appeared well. No, more than well. He appeared more vibrant and alive than we had ever seen him. And, as if he was privy to our private conversation, Jesus approached Thomas and showed Thomas his wrists and feet that bore the marks of the nails that held him to the cross. He then exposed his side for all of us to see the spear wound. Our brother Thomas then fell on his knees and expressed the sentiments for us all when he said, 'My Lord and my God.' Then our Lord instructed us to go to Galilee and await him there."

"And you went," I said.

"Yes, we went. We left that very night, and journeyed back to our home in Bethsaida with much haste, and stopping as little as possible along the way.

"Most of us were fishermen by trade, and while in Bethsaida we went out on a boat to fish. By morning we had caught nothing. On shore a man appeared who called out to us and asked if we had caught any fish. We told him we had not, and he told us to cast our nets over the right-hand side of the boat. We did as he instructed, and our nets became full. James looked at the man on shore and said to me, 'Peter, it is the Lord!'. When I looked, it was indeed Jesus. Filled with excitement, I jumped into the water and swam ashore. The others followed in the boat, and we ate and talked with him, as we had in years past. He told us we would have to return to Jerusalem and wait. It was then he entrusted us to go into all the nations and bring the good news to the world."

"What good news is that?" I asked.

"That he is risen, Tribune!" Peter replied. "That we may have eternal life in Jesus Christ. That we no longer have to fear anything, and that we can endure all, for he is with us, even until the end of time."

"A very pretty speech, Peter," I commented with disdain. "Is that how you tricked Drusus and Ruth into joining your cult?"

"You may not believe, Tribune," he said. "You never knew Jesus. Like Thomas you will not believe until the truth is right before eyes, and even then you may not believe."

These words struck me full in the face, and I knew I had heard them somewhere before. I did not wish to go further into this discussion so I put this to Peter: "Do you swear on your friend's name that you did not take his body or know where it is?"

"I do so swear," he responded, and for some reason I believed him.

"When Jesus instructed you to return here and wait, did he say what you were to wait for?" I asked.

Peter shook his head and said: "He did not say. But we trust in him and we will wait."

I turned and looked at the rest of the disciples, and I shook my head. If I were to live in this godforsaken land for the remainder of my days, I would never truly understand these people. I did not know what they expected to prove, or what they had truly seen, but I was certain nothing would come of it.

I walked across the room to the door, and turned back to them. "I am satisfied with the answers I have received here today. None of you have anything further to fear from me." Stepping through the doorway, I called back over my shoulder: "You best get this door repaired soon. I cannot guarantee that others will not come for you."

CHAPTER XX

▼

I did not sleep well that night. I had hopes Ruth would come home, but she never did. Finding the disciples had brought the investigation to a close. I had no other leads, I had not one person left to speak to. I had not found the missing body of Jesus of Nazareth, nor was I likely to. In my investigation I had uncovered corruption, plots and counterplots, bribery, murder, persecution and paranoia. I did not know how it would all look in my report. Perhaps in the morning things would look better.

When I awoke in the morning things looked just as bad or worse than when I went to sleep.

I was due to make my report to the Governor that afternoon. I was not looking forward to it. There were two ways I could submit my report to the Governor; one was to lie and try to placate Pilate, in hopes that he may recommend my transfer to Rome; and the other way was to speak the truth which just might bring the combined political weight in all Jerusalem down upon my head, thereby never having a chance to see Rome again. The choice made me sick to my stomach.

I rose from a restless sleep and dressed. I did not go out to eat, but decided to get by on a cup of wine. Most of the morning was spent preparing my written report. Before lunch I decided to see Titus and Scarus and tell them to prepare their story about the morning at the tomb, because they most probably would be called upon to support my findings. At the fortress I did not find them, nor their commander. I grew anxious. Each man I questioned told me they did not know Scarus or Titus. I found two other soldiers occupying their billets. After much searching and questioning, I eventually did come across one man who told me in hushed tones that an officer had come in the night and ordered Titus and Scarus to pack their gear, and the two of them left Jerusalem without a trace.

I felt sick to my stomach and gave up the idea of having lunch.

I left the praetorium and began walking the streets of Jerusalem. The afternoon was terribly hot. My head swam from the heat and my vitals churned. Which gate I exited the city I cannot recall, but I found myself outside the eastern wall. Turning from the wall, I faced a tall hill called the Mount of Olives. For some unknown reason, I began to walk up the hill. I walked like a man in a daze. After a time, tired in body and spirit, I came to a spot among a grove of olive trees. There I found a stone bench and sat upon it. Below me lay Jerusalem, but I could only look upon it in contempt. Oh, how I hated this city. Jerusalem was not one-tenth the city Rome was, and every time I looked at Jerusalem, it made me realize how desperately I wished to see Rome once more. What made matters worse, was the feeling that I would never again set foot in the land of my birth. My heart sank in despair and I lay my head in my hands. The only two Romans who could substantiate my report regarding the events at the tomb were now gone, spirited away in the night. I had failed in my duty to find the body of Jesus of Nazareth. It would be a black mark on my record, and would work against my efforts to have my banishment revoked.

From far outside my thoughts I became aware of a voice. Someone was speaking to me. I looked up to see a man standing close by.

"May I sit here?" he asked.

I did not answer or pay him any mind, but simply went back into my own dismal thoughts. I was aware that the man sat next to me.

"You appear troubled," he commented.

I turned and regarded the man closely. From his dress and manner I could see he was a Jew. He looked about my age, perhaps a bit older. His brown hair was long and was a shade darker than his beard. He was dressed simply, clean and neat. His clothes bespoke a man of little wealth, especially his leather sandals that were worn from much travel. I wondered why, out of the entire hillside, he came to sit next to me and interrupt my musing. I also wondered why my troubled appearance concerned him at all.

"Yes, I am troubled, and I came here to think," I told him, hoping he would understand my meaning.

"Yes," he said. "In the past I, too, have come here when troubled. It is a lovely spot."

"But not very private," I muttered.

"A man I know owns this garden. It is called Gethsemane. The name means 'oil press'. Very good oil comes from this grove. But I do not believe you came here to speak of oil."

I gave him a sidelong glance, and suspected there was hidden meaning in his words.

"No," I said, "I did not come here to speak of oil."

"But you do appear very discouraged," the man remarked. "What is it that troubles you so?"

"Why do you wish to know?" I countered.

He grinned and said: "I do not wish to know so much as you need to tell me."

I did not even consider that his words made little sense, but blurted out: "I was sent to find someone, and I could not find him."

"Whom do you seek?"

"One of your people," I told him. "A Galilean named Jesus."

"Why do you seek this man Jesus?"

"I was ordered to find him," I replied irritably. "When I am given a command, I carry it out to the end."

"Ah. You are a man of duty and responsibility."

"Yes, I am."

"But what else are you?" he asked.

"I do not understand," I replied, confused. "What else do I have to be?"

The man smiled and said: "Will performing this duty gain you anything? Is there something you wish?"

"It will give me the opportunity to return to Rome," I informed him. "That is all I wish."

"Why did you leave Rome?"

I stared coldly at the man and said: "That is none of your business."

"Is your family in Rome? Is that why you wish to return there?"

"I do not talk of my family with strangers," I stated.

"Do you talk of your family to your friends here in Jerusalem?"

"I have no friends here in Jerusalem."

"A man should have friends wherever he goes. Perhaps if you had friends here, they could help you find Jesus."

"I do not think I will ever find Jesus," I said with finality.

"Perhaps you will find him—some day."

"I need to find him now!"

"You are an impatient man."

I turned and faced him. Our eyes met and I uttered: "Some have said so."

I turned away and looked ahead. After a bout of silence I said: "I do not know for certain if the man is dead or alive. Some swear he is dead, while others swear they have seen him after his crucifixion."

"What do you believe?" he asked me.

"I do not know what to believe. I have no proof one way or another."

"Some people would not believe if the proof were right in front of them."

He said this, and I tried to recall where I had heard that before.

"Is finding this man so important?" he asked me.

"The responsibility of finding Jesus was entrusted to me by the Prefect in the name of the Emperor."

"But is finding Jesus important to you personally?" he put to me, but I was not certain what he meant.

"I must make my report to the Governor today," I said. "I am not certain what I will say."

"You appear to be an honest man," he said rising. "I am confident you will tell the truth."

He began to walk away, took two steps and turned back to face me. "If you did find the man Jesus," he proposed, "what would you say to him?"

I was briefly flummoxed by his question. After thinking about it, I said: "If I did find Jesus, I suppose I would ask him if he were indeed the Son of God."

"And if he said he were the Son of God, would you believe him?"

I shook my head and said: "I do not know."

The man smiled, turned, and without so much as a farewell, he walked off up the hill.

I looked up at the position of the sun, and calculated that it was time to go back to Jerusalem and make my report to the Governor.

CHAPTER XXI

▼

Back in my quarters I dressed in my best toga, and, picking up my report, I started for my meeting with Pontius Pilate.

It was a short wait in the small atrium before I was announced, then shown into the audience chamber. I expected to see Pilate sitting upon his chair, of course, but I was quite surprised to see Joseph Caiaphas and Herod Antipas also present.

Pilate dismissed every guard and servant until only the four of us remained in the room.

"It is my wish that the high priest and tetrarch be present to hear your report, Tribune," Pilate said to me with no emotion or expression. "Since the matter does involve their people, I thought it prudent that they are informed of what you have learned."

I looked from one to the other in turn. They reminded me of three vultures sitting in a tree waiting for some old mule to die so they might swoop down and rip it to pieces.

"You may proceed with your report, Tribune Maximus," Pontius Pilate said blandly.

I looked at the rolled up scroll in my right hand, and decided not to read it, but to make my report from memory.

"The first step in my investigation was to visit the tomb where Jesus was interred," I began. "Through an intense study of the tomb I concluded no one could escape a sealed tomb without aid from the outside."

Pilate regarded me quizzically. "What was the purpose of this study, Tribune?" he asked. "Did you truly believe the man was capable of walking out of his own tomb?"

"My study was based on the hypothesis that the man in question was not dead when he was placed in the tomb."

As I said this, all three men looked amazed, and before any could ask a question I continued.

"While at the tomb I came across two men who aided in the interment of Jesus; Joseph of Arimathea, and a Pharisee named Nicodemus."

Recognition of these names was reflected in the high priest's face, and he asked me: "Do you believe these two men had anything to do with the disappearance of the dead Galilean?"

"No, I do not," I replied. "Neither of these men had the physical capability of moving the stone from the entrance of the tomb individually nor together."

"They may have had help," Herod volunteered.

"I overheard a private conversation between the two men, and both were surprised at the disappearance of the body," I informed them. "My next step was to speak with the centurion who oversaw the crucifixion. His name was Lucius Drusus. Though he did swear to me the Galilean was dead when his body was removed from the cross, my suspicions led me to believe that Jesus was actually alive at the time."

"What in the centurion's account led you to that conclusion?" Pilate asked me.

"By his own admission the centurion told me that he felt pity for the Galilean, and did not inflict the usual amount of punishment on the prisoner. This was also verified by the soldiers under his command. Even when it was time to issue the final blow that would ensure the death of the condemned, Drusus kept his men from breaking the legs of Jesus. This in itself was suspicious, added to the fact it was on the centurion's word alone that you, Prefect, released the body to Joseph of Arimathea."

"So you suspect the centurion attempted to deceive us?" Pilate asked.

"I did at first," I admitted. "But something the centurion said made me think otherwise."

"What did he say?" The Prefect wanted to know.

"According to his account, some very strange things took place during the crucifixion."

"What things?" Pontius Pilate queried.

"At the moment of Jesus's death, the sky turned dark and the earth shook."

"Is that all?" Herod Antipas spoke with his head thrust forward expectantly.

"Tribune," Pilate began, "you can hardly expect us to believe that a change in the weather is *argumentum ad rem*, or could possibly cause all this..." Pilate let the sentence trail off, not knowing how to describe the cause and effect.

"Lucius Drusus also had an excellent opportunity to observe Jesus before his death," I said. "The centurion stated to me that he believed Jesus was a righteous man."

"Tribune..."

"And he also believed he was the Son of God!" I said interrupting Pilate.

This last statement caused the room to grow surprisingly silent.

After an uneasy exchange of glances with Herod and Caiaphas, Pilate said: "I would speak with this centurion."

I was afraid he would say that. This morning I had decided not to reveal to anyone that I had found Lucius Drusus, even if it meant that this part of my report could not be verified.

"The centurion has been missing for the last few days," I told them, and I noticed a satisfying smile touched the lips of Joseph Caiaphas.

Pontius Pilate audibly cleared his throat in an attempt to gain everyone's attention before he spoke. "What is next on your report, Tribune Maximus?"

"Next I spoke with the Roman guards who were present in the Garden of Gethsemane when Jesus was arrested. They were also present at the man's crucifixion, and they guarded his burial place at the behest of the high priest."

The eyes of Caiaphas darted to me, then to Pilate, and back to me again.

Pilate picked up on the high priest's distress, and he addressed me authoritatively: "The guards were ordered by *me* to stand watch at the tomb, Tribune."

"At the high priest's request," I added.

Pilate did not care to respond to this, but said coldly, "Continue with your report, Tribune."

"My first interview with the four guards was of little help, mainly because they lied to me regarding the events at the tomb of Jesus two days after the man's burial. Their original story was that after imbibing on a goatskin of wine, the guards grew tired and fell asleep at their watch, and while they slept the followers of Jesus came in the night and made off with the body. After some...persuasion, one of the four guards decided to tell me the true events that took place at the tomb. He told me that early in the morning the earth shook violently and the guards fell to the ground, where, for a time, they were held in the grip of a paralysis. They were aware, however, that a blinding white light emanated from the tomb. Two Hebrew women passed by them unaffected, stayed briefly at the tomb and left. When the guards were free of their affliction, they discovered the tomb was empty. Immediately the guards left the scene to report these events to the high priest, Joseph Caiaphas."

I could almost feel the intense agitation being given off by the high priest. I suspected Caiaphas might not have told Pilate I approached him and accused him of bribing the guards to lie, with hopes that I would not go ahead and report my findings. Now they were out in the open, and I had to see it to the end.

"When the guards reported what they had seen, the high priest gave them money to say the body of Jesus was taken by his followers."

"Your excellency," Caiaphas spoke up, "I find it insulting to stand here and listen to these false allegations. The Tribune has accused me of wrongdoing before. Perhaps it would be simpler if the Tribune explained how he *persuaded* the guard to relate this fantastic, but untrue, story. He beat the guard until the man said what the Tribune wished to hear."

"Perhaps the high priest should explain how he knows what I did?" I countered, revealing my contempt.

"Tribune Maximus," Pilate addressed me sternly. He was doing his best to keep the high priest from appearing in a bad light. "Much of this may be settled if we could speak with the four guards in question."

I regarded Pilate suspiciously. He spoke these words as if he already knew what I was about to say.

"None of the guards are available," I stated. "Two are dead and—"

"Dead!" exclaimed Pontius Pilate.

"Yes, your excellency." I did not believe the Prefect was as surprised as he appeared.

"What of the dead guards?" Herod queried. "Do you know how they died?"

Pilate motioned me to respond and I did so. "The young guard, Flavius, who told me the truth about the events at the tomb, was killed by his brother-soldier, Marius. Marius killed Flavius for revealing their secret to me, which they all swore they would never tell to anyone. Soon after, Marius was found dead."

"How did Marius die?" Pilate wanted to know.

"He was murdered," I said simply, and hoped to leave it at that, but Herod would not.

"Do you have any idea who murdered Marius?" Herod said, and his tone made me believe he knew or suspected I had killed Marius.

"I have no idea who killed Marius," I lied.

"I heard he was murdered by a Roman Tribune," Caiaphas commented innocently.

"And would you care to explain where you heard that?" I said with some vehemence "Or is the high priest in the habit of spreading rumours he knows nothing about?"

"That is enough, Tribune Maximus," Pilate said to me. "The high priest is our guest, and you will not address him in that manner again. Is that understood?"

"Yes, your excellency," I said.

"Now, before anyone else makes another unsubstantiated claim, I would speak with the two remaining guards."

"Neither of those guards is available," I remarked. "The two of them are missing."

Pilate endeavoured to look surprised and disappointed. Now I was certain he had ordered Titus and Scarus transferred out of Jerusalem.

"Well, Tribune," the Prefect said smugly, "it would appear that most of your witnesses are dead or missing. Is there no one who can substantiate your report?"

"There are the followers of Jesus," I stated rather reluctantly. "They can verify part of my report."

Pilate did not look impressed. He said: "I am not willing to take the word of these people." Neither Caiaphas nor Herod appreciated this remark. Both of them knew to whom the term *these people* referred. Pilate continued. "Is there no *Roman* who can substantiate your report?"

"No Prefect," I answered, then added: "No one else, except perhaps…"

"Yes," Pilate said rather impatiently. "Except whom?"

"There is yourself, Prefect," I told him.

An indignant look crept across the Governor's face. "I am afraid I do not understand, Tribune Maximus. What have I got to do with this entire matter?"

"May I remind you, Prefect, that under your orders the man Jesus was condemned, crucified, and buried. You gave Joseph of Arimathea permission to bury the body. Roman guards were stationed at the tomb under your orders. These same soldiers were ordered by you to accompany Temple guards to arrest Jesus, which proves collusion between yourself and Caiaphas before Jesus was even brought before you. It was your authority, and your authority alone that was duped and used by these two men." I pointed an accusing finger at Herod and Caiaphas. "They did not wish to do away with the man Jesus, so they tricked Rome into doing it for them. And what is more to the point—"

"Tribune, *vir sapit qui pauca loquitur!*" Pilate proclaimed harshly. He looked about the room anxiously, like an animal with hunters on all sides. After a time he spoke. "Tribune Maximus, you have insulted my noble guests, and have brought accusations against them with no proof. Protocol dictates that I insist you apologize to them at once."

I stared back at Pilate.

"Tribune, you will apologize."

I stood unmoving.

"Tribune Maximus, I am ordering you to apologize."

I turned in the direction of Herod and Caiaphas. The utter contempt I felt for these two men was obvious to everyone in the room. Somehow I worked my mouth to say: "I apologize."

"Very well then," Pilate spoke, his tone less harsh, and he turned to Herod and Caiaphas and said: "My honoured guests, please accept my apologies along with those of Tribune Maximus. I will not insist you remain to hear anything further." Pilate called for his guards. Two of them entered the room and he addressed them. "Please escort these gentlemen out."

Herod and Caiaphas exchanged confused looks, then turned and bowed to Pilate before they left the room with the guards at their heels. Pilate and I were left alone. The Prefect refused to look at me, but his gaze remained fixed upon his hands that rested in his lap. Finally he spoke.

"So, Tribune, you have given up all hope of ever returning to Rome," he said still staring at his hands.

"Do not threaten me," I responded.

"You will not use that tone with me, Tribune," he came back with controlled anger as he regarded me briefly, then looked away again. "One word from me and you will never see Rome again. You have done little to ingratiate yourself into my good graces. Those two men are friends of the state. Did you think I would simply allow you to say whatever you wished?"

"You were afraid what I would say next. That is why you had Caiaphas and Herod leave the room."

"And what did I fear you would say?" Pilate asked contemptuously.

"I was about to say that you went along with Herod and Caiaphas in their plan to eliminate Jesus because the three of you have been stealing money from the Temple treasury. That is how you have been paying for the new aqueduct."

I saw Pilate's already pale face drain of whatever colour remained. His bloodless lips moved as if he were about to say something, but no words came out. I decided to continue.

"Did you know that as high priest, Caiaphas has the authority to condemn any of his own people to death? He does. Reliable sources have confirmed it. Even Herod could have executed the man, but he did not. Does it not strike you strange that Caiaphas would lie to you and say that in all of Jerusalem only you had that authority? You may have known it all along, or perhaps you did not, but you decided to do what they were asking you to do. I do not believe you were sanguine about the idea. You genuinely tried to spare Jesus the crucifixion, and I do not believe it was only because your wife advised you not to get involved in the affair. Perhaps in your heart you believed what Caiaphas and Herod were attempting to do to Jesus was wrong, and you may have wanted to spare his life because you believed him innocent, or merely because your wife asked you to. I do not know." Here Pilate tried not to look shocked that I knew the events regarding his wife. "You did everything but release him, which was within your authority. You even tried to pass the deed off to Herod, but he would not take it upon himself to do it, so Herod sent Jesus back to you. When Jesus was crucified and you ordered his *titulus* to read, 'the King of the Jews', you were sending Herod a message. You did not want him to forget how tenuous his position was as tetrarch. Afterwards, Herod did everything he could to stay in your good graces. I know the two of you have been spending more time together.

"For some reason, the Hebrews had not wanted the responsibility of killing Jesus, so they got Rome to do it for them. The money from the Temple treasury was now a two-edged sword in their hands. You would comply with their wishes, lest the truth regarding your misappropriation of Temple funds be exposed and word of this gets back to Rome. That is why you fear me. That is why you fear my report." I held up the papers in my hand.

Pilate did something he rarely did; he looked directly at me. "*Qualis pater talis filius*," he declared without rancour. "Like father like son." I endeavoured not to take it as a compliment, nor an insult. "You have that same stubborn quality as your father. Has anyone ever told you that you are a stubborn man?"

"Some have said so."

"Yes, I am certain. You must guard against being too stubborn, Tribune. Your stubbornest borders on obstinacy, and it will be your undoing."

"It aids me in my service to the Emperor," I said with more that a hint of defiance.

"You may think you know everything, Tribune, but you do not."

"I know what I need to know," I said confidently. "I know that Jesus was more than Caiaphas would have us believe. Caiaphas and his ilk felt threatened, fearing a loss of power and prestige. When people began to refer to Jesus as the King of the Jews, Herod Antipas felt threatened in the same way. One man a religious leader, the other a political leader. In order to keep the *status quo*, they both plotted against Jesus *malo animo*. The high priests and elders feared Jesus might be something more than a mere man—though they knew not what. Perhaps Jesus possessed full knowledge of *arcanum arcanorum*—the secret of secrets. At any rate, the Jewish elders did not wish to risk any kind of reprisal for his death, so they got you to do it.

"I know that one of Caiaphas's servants was struck with a sword the night they went to arrest Jesus, and Jesus healed the man's wound. Now this man cannot be found, and Caiaphas denies he even exists.

"I know that something strange and unnatural occurred at the tomb. I know that the high priest gave the guards who were at the tomb money to bear false witness."

Pilate nervously wrung his hands and I said: "I know that no matter how many times you wash your hands, you will never be able to wash the man's blood from them."

Pontius Pilate started, and quickly raised his hands before his eyes. It was an uncontrollable gesture, and he glared angrily, knowing he had betrayed himself.

"Proof, Tribune!" Pilate proclaimed bitterly. "Where is your proof of all this? These statements are meaningless without proof."

"You would not believe even if the proof were before your eyes," I stated boldly.

"I know where the centurion Lucius Drusus is, but I am not going to reveal it," I spoke. "I also know where Jesus's disciples are hiding, but I am not willing to give up their location either. But it is important that you know I will use them to support my claims if I ever find myself *a fronte praecipitium a tergo lupi.*"

"You do not consider yourself in that position now?" Pontius Pilate asked me slowly, and his words carried a hint of a threat.

"No. I do not believe you will take any steps against me. The report I plan on sending to Rome will simply state that I did not find the body of Jesus—which is true. My report will also state that I do not believe his disciples made off with the body of Jesus—which is also true. I am certain this matter will all be forgotten in a matter of months. The incident involves Jewish beliefs and Jewish law. It all falls under Jewish jurisdiction, since they have the right to settle matters of their own religion. I trust Rome will not wish to pursue this and we will not be persecuting Jesus's disciples. I am confident neither Caiaphas nor Herod will bring any charges or complaints against you. Their hands are far from clean in this matter, and I am certain they wish to see the entire affair over with."

Pontius Pilate sat silently for some time trying to digest all I had told him. In his mind he weighed his options and attempted to foresee contingencies. In the end he said: "Yes, well, it would seem that our business is concluded. Your report,

Tribune." Pilate held out his hand. I placed my written report in his hand. He stood and walked about the room scanning the document. Stopping by a brazier, he dropped the document into the fire. I stood where I was and watched it burn.

"The report I forward to Rome will state that the Centurion Drusus fell into duplicity with the followers of Jesus of Nazareth, and allowed them to take his body down from the cross before the man was dead. The soldiers guarding the tomb were given a drink that caused them to see bizarre sights and while they were incapacitated, the body was stolen. The man Jesus and his followers have fled Jerusalem and are in hiding."

"No one will believe that," I stated.

"And is your story any more believable, Tribune Maximus?"

"What is to stop me from submitting my own report?"

"There is that stubborn streak again, Tribune. For once be smart. This report bears many of your original theories. Your name will be on it with your cooperation or not. The Emperor will see this as a favourable report, and you will find yourself one step closer to Rome.

"Though you were not completely successfully in the assignment you were given, I am satisfied with your performance, and my report will state the same. This matter is hereby concluded and we need never speak of it again. *Dixi*! Good day, Tribune."

CHAPTER XXII

▼

Ruth did not come home the day of my interview with Pontius Pilate. She did not come home the day after that, or the day after that. After several more days I resigned myself to the realization that she was never coming back. I had lost her to the Jesus-ites forever. I hoped for her sake that there was not some female ritual like the one Lucius Drusus had to endure.

I found myself returning to the Mount of Olives every morning. Secretly I hoped I would meet again the Jewish man I spoke with the first time I was there, but I was never to see him again. I had not even asked him his name.

Then, one day, as I sat on the same bench where I sat every morning and I stared down upon Jerusalem, someone approached and said: "May I sit here?" I was certain it was the man I had met before, and I turned expectantly only to see:

"Marcus!" I exclaimed. "What are you doing here?"

"I was at the Temple Mount," Marcus Malachi said, a trifle out of breath and ruddy-cheeked, "and I just happened to look out and I saw you pass along outside the wall of the city. I decided to follow you." Marcus looked about our surroundings. "It seems like a nice, secluded spot you have chosen, and no one is likely see us together."

"Please, sit down," I said to him.

"I was surprised to see you come here," Marcus commented. "I did not imagine you were the thoughtful, reflective type."

"It is a nice, quiet spot," I remarked, looking around at the peaceful grove of olive trees.

"It is that," Marcus agreed. "I do not remember ever coming here before."

"It does not seem as hot here as it does in the city," I said, and added sombrely: "This is where he came that night, and was arrested."

"So, you still think about him," Marcus said.

"It was one of my few failures, and I do not suffer failures well."

"Few of us do," Marcus conceded.

"Have you heard anything from the Jesus-ites?" I asked.

"No," Marcus spoke slowly. "They have been keeping very quiet as of late."

"Just as well," I responded. "I am certain everything will get back to normal, and we will very likely never hear from them again."

"Perhaps," he said. "But they certainly did have some very interesting beliefs."

"You're not considering becoming one, are you?" I asked, half serious.

"You know me better than to ask," Marcus replied, taking no offence at my question.

I looked down on Jerusalem. Somehow it looked different from up here. The streets did not appear as crowded and dirty. One could not smell the odour of people and animals pressed together within its walls. From here one could almost feel far removed from the politics and religion and intrigue.

"I have the awful feeling that I will never see Rome again," I found myself admitting in a low voice. Tears welled in my eyes. I tried to smile despite this, but I could not get my lips to obey.

Marcus looked at me with sympathy and asked: "Do you not think Emperor Tiberias will allow you to return to Rome?" I shrugged my shoulders then Marcus said hopefully: "Perhaps Pontius Pilate will speak to the Emperor on your behalf."

"The Prefect has his own difficulties at the moment," I revealed. "Rome is questioning some of his practices. Pilate believes I sent a secret report on him to Rome, and he is not conducive to doing me any favours. If only I had simply given him what he wanted. I could have made a report he approved of, but instead I antagonized him by bringing accusations against him."

"Why did you?"

"What?" I said. His question caught me by surprise. I had never thought about why I had done it. "I suppose I did it because it was the truth."

"Some men value truth more than their own personal desires."

I grunted at Marcus's remark. It was of little consolation. I said, "Now I shall never get out of this place."

Marcus gave a little grunt of his own and stated: "Jerusalem is not that bad a place to live. You get used to it in time. I know I have."

"Marcus," I said as a brilliant sun ascended a very blue sky. "You never truly explained to me why you were banished from Thrace."

"No?" he uttered as if he could not recall clearly. I shook my head, and he said: "I suppose I was saving that story for a rainy day when we were stuck inside, and we had exhausted all other subjects on which to speak."

I accepted his answer and said: "You never asked me about the circumstances surrounding my banishment from Rome."

"No," he said again. "I thought that you would tell me when the time was right."

As I looked at him, we both smiled a wry, knowing smile, and I said: "Marcus, I believe it is time."

Afterword

This story is, of course, a work of fiction. Though the story was based on the four Gospels, other references were used to help preserve the historical accuracy of the times and place.

The basis of this story is not to assign guilt or blame to *any* group. The research for this book presented all the elements of a good mystery not unlike the classic 1940's hard-boiled detective story. No anti-Semitism was intended, nor do I hope any will arise out of this work. Since the death of Jesus Christ was prophesied, and was, I believe, the will of God, no one should be blamed for Christ's death which was ordained, necessary and could not be prevented.

Though I have striven for historical accuracy, any and all errors found in the story are to be placed at my door, and the reader will, I hope, forgive me.

Stephen Gaspar
Windsor, Ontario

0-595-31459-7